MONSTER, HE WROTE

FULL MOON FEVER
BOOK 1

DOUG MOLITOR

THE ALTADENA
PRESS LLC

The Altadena Press
www.thealtadenapress.com

Cover photographer: Gary M. Black
Model: Lisa McCluskey
Cover Design by Kristin Bryant at Kristin Design

Publication date: July 2024

Third Edition

ISBN: 978-1-965057-10-0 (E-BOOK)
ISBN: 978-1-965057-11-7 (PRINT BOOK)

PRAISE FOR DOUG MOLITOR

"You couldn't ask for a finer guide to the future, or the past, than Doug Molitor. Having so thoroughly enjoyed his 'Memoirs of a Time Traveler,' the next book I read is, without a doubt, going to be his 'Memoirs of a Time Traveler' again."

— LARRY GELBART, *M*A*S*H, TOOTSIE, CITY OF ANGELS, A FUNNY THING HAPPENED ON THE WAY TO THE FORUM*

"*Full Moon Fever* is a paranormal mystery and a romantic comedy, all-in-one. Sit back with a glass of Holy Water, a loaf of garlic bread and a rare stake, and enjoy the ride."

— CHRISTIANA MILLER, AUTHOR, *SOMEBODY TELL AUNT TILLIE SHE'S DEAD*

CONTENTS

"There are horrors beyond life's edge that we do not suspect, and once in a while man's evil prying calls them just within our range."

— *Howard Phillips Lovecraft*

1

THE HIGH PRIEST

"DEATH SHALL COME ON SWIFT WINGS FOR HE who dares defile this tomb," read the curse inscribed on the ancient seal, and had Professor Bramwell heeded its warning, this story would be far shorter than it is. But Bramwell's place in history depended upon whether beyond the door lay the untouched tomb of the Pharaoh Mentuhotep II.

The light of the rising moon revealed that above the dire hieroglyphs was carved the jackal-headed image of Anubis, the Egyptian god of the dead. The clay of the seal had dried four millennia ago, encasing the knotted, rotted rope that had closed this tomb, circa 2010 B.C.

The crumbling papyrus scroll he'd bought in a Luxor bazaar was no fake, after all, for it had led him to this hidden cave in the Valley of the Kings, where he had now found his life's goal.

"Professor?" Harry Fletcher, Bramwell's brash young American student, removed his pith helmet and mopped his brow. "It's late. Are we going in?"

"Yes. Yes, of course. Hold up the lantern." The professor gripped his student's elbow and moved it up, as if adjusting a piece of equipment—an irritating habit that the younger man had learned to tolerate.

Bramwell neatly cut the seal off the door. There were only the two of them to witness this historic event. Their superstitious workers had quit *en masse*, as soon as they had seen the dread mark of the jackal.

The dirt-encrusted wooden door swung inward. Out came the faint, foul odor of decay. The two Egyptologists moved down the dim passage, which widened out to a burial chamber. At one end lay a sarcophagus.

In one sense, they were fortunate: The chamber was untouched. Yet their hearts sank, for there was no gold. This was no pharaoh's tomb.

Then the professor saw the seal on the sarcophagus. "Good Lord," he breathed. "This isn't Mentuhotep. It's Sethis."

"The court magician?" said Fletcher.

"He was quite a bit more than that if the scroll is to be believed," replied the professor. "Counselor. High priest. Sorcerer of great power."

The professor again moved Fletcher's arm higher, for better light as he unsealed the sarcophagus.

Fletcher fumed. "Rubbish. It said Sethis could sever an enemy's arm with a wave of his hand. That he could raise the dead."

"Are you so certain he couldn't?"

"Come now, Professor, this is the nineteenth century. We live in the age of science."

"Harry, the Egyptians forged metal alloys we have yet to duplicate. Their embalming techniques are still a puzzle. Who's to say they did not possess some occult knowledge that our science does not yet admit?"

"Then why are you defying their curse?"

Bramwell set the seal aside. "Because I'm not some bloody heathen. Now, give me a hand."

The two men lifted off the wooden lid, set it on the floor, and gazed at the occupant.

The mummy was remarkably tall and had clearly been a man of powerful build. The scent of sandalwood mixed with a weird stench...not decay, exactly, but something more eldritch.

"I've never seen such a well-preserved mummy. But isn't this odd? See how the face and limbs are exposed, not wrapped in the final layer of linen. And the organs in jars are not here. This was not a complete mummification. In fact...good Lord, I think the poor fellow was buried alive," Bramwell said.

"Then he wasn't much of a sorcerer, was he?"

"He may have been drugged beforehand. And awoke to find himself sealed in the sarcophagus." The professor shuddered at the thought.

But what drew Fletcher's eyes was the mummy's ornate breastplate. "Look at the neckpiece! Solid gold, from the look of it!"

"I shouldn't be surprised. The scroll does give one a distinct impression of Sethis' vanity. It depicts him wearing as much gold as the pharaoh himself. And he does seem to have been a strapping, handsome fellow. Classical features."

Fletcher frowned at the withered face, dubious.

"But look here, Harry!" Once more, the professor adjusted Fletcher's arm higher. Then he read, his lips murmuring the ancient Egyptian words, as he ran his finger along the hieroglyphs on the bottom rim of the neckpiece.

Fletcher could feel his own heart thudding. But it was not fear that thrilled him. It was opportunity.

The professor tapped the pictograms. "This is a spell.

Whoever entombed Sethis wasn't taking any chances on offending the gods. They buried his curse with him." He smiled. "I daresay the museum will be exceedingly grateful for this find."

Fletcher scoffed. "Thirty years you've slaved for them. What gratitude did they ever show?"

The old man turned to his protégé, surprised. "What are you saying?"

Fletcher locked eyes with Bramwell. "I know a collector who'd pay us a million dollars for this piece, no questions asked."

Bramwell stared back. At last, he spoke. "We will forget that you ever said that."

"Professor, be reasonable. You could retire. Or you could fund your own expeditions!"

"We are not tomb robbers! This find belongs to posterity," said Bramwell with finality. He turned away and bent over the mummy, resuming his inspection.

In that moment, Fletcher felt the crowbar seem to take on a life of its own, rising high overhead, and then plunging down with ferocious force. Fletcher felt cranial bone give way to forged metal, which bogged down in soft matter underneath.

Fletcher released his grip. The gory crowbar hit the stone, and the clank echoed from the tomb walls.

The corpse of Fletcher's slain mentor lay at his feet, but it seemed no more real to him than the fallen troops in the tomb wall paintings: just another victim in history's inexorable march.

Fletcher gingerly took hold of the neckpiece. It was dense—pure gold, as he'd guessed. But it would not come loose. It seemed to be fastened behind the mummy's neck.

He could have reached behind the mummy and untied

or unhooked or whatever needed doing, but he was loath to touch the filthy thing. Instead, he gave the golden ornament a fierce upward tug.

The neckpiece came loose. As did the head, which flew at Fletcher, bounced off his shirt, and rolled across the floor.

Fletcher frantically swatted the mummy dust off himself and shivered in revulsion. Then he turned his attention to his gleaming prize.

Wait, what was that behind him?

He whirled.

There was no one there. Except the head of Sethis, which had come to rest by the tomb wall. Facing him.

It looked so absurd sitting by itself on the stone floor, Fletcher could not suppress a high-pitched laugh.

"Well, it's no great loss, High Priest. You may have been handsome once, but this neckpiece deserves a prettier face than yours."

As he turned away, Fletcher glimpsed in his peripheral vision something from the mummy's puckered eye sockets.

A glint of bright crimson? A reflection? He looked back. No. The eyes were closed. As they had to be. Mummified flesh might last four thousand years in this parched climate, but eyes? Impossible. And in any event, no human eye could have glowed as red as he had just imagined.

He was tired. That was it. Overwork had taken its toll.

His gaze turned back to his treasure. It was perfect. Not so much as a scratch.

Once again, he felt fingers grab his arm. Irritation got the better of him.

"Professor, I wish you would not..." Fletcher stopped.

It was not the late professor's hand that gripped his forearm...but that of the headless mummy.

Horror as he had never before known engulfed him, but

he was helpless to move, as the mummy's torso rose from the sarcophagus and its other hand reached for his throat.

He had time for only one scream, but it was as high and as loud as any sound he had made in his life.

It was noon when a young Egyptologist named Carter made his way down the passageway to the burial chamber. That morning Bramwell's foreman had told him of the find, and at once Carter had been seized by an inexplicable premonition that his colleagues were in mortal danger.

Entering the tomb, he held his torch high. A mummified head lay in the far corner. Also, a freshly dead body. Probably Bramwell. But that must wait. First, Carter felt compelled to see what was in that sarcophagus.

Imagine his surprise when he looked upon the mummy and saw, set off by the golden neckpiece, the handsome face of his friend Fletcher...HIS HEAD TORN OFF!

And thirty children screamed as one.

2

THE MONSTER MAN

He'd designed it as the perfect campfire ghost story, like *The Golden Arm* or *The Walking Coffin*. Only his tale had the classy retro touch of a mummy antagonist. And it didn't end on a groaner. Jeez, the walking casket that is halted because Luden's Cough Drops always stop the coughin'? Yikes. Pre-school stuff.

The problem was, after the scream, you're supposed to get a relieved laugh.

But the kids sitting on the foam-rubber jigsaw puzzle mat were neither relieved nor laughing. Petrified and jaws agape would be closer to the mark.

Drake Callahan brushed unruly hair off his brow and tried to prime the pump with a hearty laugh of his own, but it died away, having elicited nothing but more saucer-eyed stares from his charges. Possibly, they thought he'd gone crazy. Drake gave them his best disarming, brainy-slacker grin. No dice.

All right, maybe a decapitating mummy was a bit intense for this age group. He made a mental note to go with *The Walking Coffin* next Halloween.

"Now, come on, kids, it's just a story," he cajoled. "You asked for a scary one."

"Not *that* scary!" protested Madison, a disagreeable tot under the best of circumstances.

Her pal Tyrone nodded his head in furious agreement. "I *hate* story time!"

The reviews were in, and they were not good.

Suddenly, just beyond his range of vision, Drake sensed a shape looming behind him. *Impossible*, he thought. Not the principal. She was off campus this afternoon.

Someone cleared her throat.

Drake turned and tried not to flinch at seeing Dr. Zylpha Benson, six-feet-two and hawk-beaked, glaring at him from the doorway in a manner that Anubis, guide of the dead, would have admired.

Beside the principal stood Nicole Finley, the love of Drake's life, chestnut-haired, heartbreakingly lovely...and at the moment, utterly mortified.

"Mr. Callahan, may I speak to you?" asked Dr. Benson.

Drake nodded and rose. "Okay, kids, everyone get your pillows and lie down; it's naptime."

"I'm never gonna sleep again!" vowed Madison.

"Me neither!" chimed in Tyrone and several others.

Drake came over to the doorway, which was draped on both sides with orange paper pumpkins bearing the students' names.

Dr. Benson beckoned him out into the hallway, keeping her voice low. "And *you* are never going to substitute here again."

Keeping one foot inside the door, Drake looked back at the kids lying on the rug. They had formed a tight defensive circle like a wagon train.

"They asked for a Halloween story," he whispered.

"Your job is to teach them to count and to finger paint, not make them have nightmares or wet their pants."

"Nobody wet their..." Drake paused and glanced back at the jigsaw mat to be sure.

"I heard the end of your story. It was completely inappropriate for kindergarteners."

"Dr. Benson, kids love a good, safe scare. When I was their age, our teacher read to us from *Grimm's Fairy Tales*. We loved it! Kids shoving old ladies into ovens, grandmas devoured by wolves..."

"Which is why *those* stories are not read here, either!"

Nicole was giving Drake her subtle "don't-push-it" look, but he was fired up now, determined to make the case for enriching children's imaginations.

"Haven't you ever seen *The Wizard of Oz*? Well, what is it that you remember most from that movie? I'll tell you what: how scary that Wicked Witch..."

Drake trailed off, belatedly noticing Dr. Benson's strong resemblance to Margaret Hamilton. Nicole leapt into the ensuing pause.

"Drake's a scholar. His stories are an education. I know they're a little scary, but you'll never meet another teacher who knows as much folklore and history as Drake."

Drake nodded. "This story was based on extensive research on ancient Egypt. It's all true."

Dr. Benson intensified her glare.

"Well," he admitted, "except for the part about the mummy coming back to life and killing a guy. But don't you see?" he persisted. "Fairy tales, horror stories, they're like dress rehearsals for those inevitable times in our lives when we will experience fear of the unknown. They prepare us, they strengthen us, and they teach us lessons."

Dr. Benson drew herself up, adding another inch. "I have

a lesson of my own for you. Since you see chronicling monsters as some kind of noble calling, I suggest that you make *that* your profession. Write horror stories for adults instead of scaring children!"

"It's funny you should say that..." Drake tiptoed back into the classroom, reached into his laptop bag, and emerged with a trade paperback, six by nine inches, half an inch thick, with a lurid illustration of a shambling, stitch-scarred creature lurching out of a graveyard. In red "Famous Monsters" font, it identified itself as *THE MONSTER MAN by Drake Callahan.*

He held it out to Dr. Benson. "My first novel."

Dr. Benson remained immobile.

"Would you like me to autograph it?" he asked.

"Well, it was worth a shot," Drake told Nicole as they walked to the faculty parking lot.

"If she'd had a gun, I bet she'd have agreed," said Nicole.

THE LATE EDWIN JARRETT

L ISA CHEN CHECKED HER PHONE: HER BLIND date was now fifteen minutes overdue.

The sun had gone down an hour ago, and it was dark out on Franklin Avenue. There was a bright glow rising behind the Hollywood Hills. Normally, this was a promise of scenic nighttime views and romance, but this summer and fall, it had taken on a grimmer meaning: Tonight there would probably be another gory homicide somewhere in the City of the Angels. And the odds were now eight-to-one that it would occur within walking distance of here.

Every month since July, as the lunar orb waxed in the sky, the Full Moon Killer became the talk of the town. If the town knew all the facts that the police were withholding, it wouldn't be talking, it would be screaming in terror.

The details in the media were horrific enough: nine Angelenos torn apart over the last three months. Always on the night of the full moon, or on the night immediately prior to or after it. Always in a secluded location far from security cameras. There were unconfirmed rumors that the victims had an organized crime connection, which was the only reason civilians still walked the streets, feeling they were relatively safe.

They were wrong.

What the media had not reported, and had not been told, was these were not gangland slayings. Also withheld was that the police could find no evidence that a knife or other weapon or tool had been used.

Which to Lisa's mind left just one weapon: teeth.

But that was only an assumption: the coroner's reports were sealed—eyes-only for the top police brass, who deemed this disturbing information too likely to cause mass hysteria if released. Lisa would have given a year's salary to get a peek at those autopsy reports.

And Edwin was now seventeen minutes late. She had a sinking feeling about this date. But what the hell, she was here and had nothing else scheduled for tonight. She finished her coffee, opened her laptop, and scrolled through the details of the Full Moon victims in chronological order:

July 30th: Malcolm Moberly, 26. Officially unemployed, but known to the LAPD as a mid-level drug dealer; he was found slaughtered in his white Lamborghini, parked on a roadside in Griffith Park. He had twenty-five hundred dollars in cash in his wallet, and methamphetamine of equivalent worth was found in his glove compartment. A loaded but unused gun lay by his corpse.

July 31st: Baruch Alef, 56. A diamond merchant, whose remains were discovered in the garage of his Laughlin Park mansion, just a precious stone's throw from the Cecil B. DeMille estate. The target of a federal money-laundering probe, he had cash and two pistols on him and ten thousand dollars in gems in a blood-drenched briefcase beside his body.

August 1st: Art Dobrin, 39, private investigator known for his pitbull tactics in defense of his mob clients. He was attacked at the back door of his Atwater Village office. No sign of anything being stolen, except that Mr. Dobrin's .357 Magnum was in his trunk, and he was short two fingers.

There had been a four-week respite, and then...

August 28th: Danny Ho, 56, Hong Kong businessman, and the reputed Dragon Head of the Los Angeles triad was fished out, his clothes and his flesh ripped to shreds, from his red-stained swimming pool off Beachwood Canyon.

August 29th: Paul Gates III, 49, rap music mogul and one-time person of interest in the decade-old cold-case slaying of his former partner, had bled out into the parking lot drain outside his Hollywood recording studio.

August 30th: Gail Franklin, 37, dentist and Internet-infamous big game hunter, was found in the trophy room of her Los Feliz mansion, her own severed head unfortunately not intact enough to mount beside those of an elephant, a rhino, and a lion she had bagged on recent safaris.

Up through the murder of Danny Ho, the LAPD had been working under the theory that these were assassinations committed by an unidentified crime organization that was making a move into Los Angeles. The idea was that the high profile nature of the victims, the disinterest in easy thefts, and the savagery of the killings all meant some new player was sending a message to local mobsters. Some of the older, more cynical cops would say the killer had been doing their job for them.

But Gates had no known connection to any organized gang, and the slain dentist was quickly cleared of any such suspicion. She just liked killing things and, like all the others, was well equipped for it.

With the city already on the edge of panic, the powers that be decided now was not the time to dispel the rumors of a gang war. The brass clamped a news blackout on the identifications of further victims.

Another four-week break, and then on the first full moon, the pattern completely broke down:

September 27th: Roosevelt Wilson, former Navy SEAL, former employee of Blackwater/Xie, considered the best bodyguard in Hollywood, was unable to guard his own body from whoever ripped out his throat and left him bleeding into the Silver Lake reservoir.

Wilson was definitely not mobbed-up. On the contrary, he had a great working relationship with the LAPD and his sterling reputation was unquestioned. Then again, so was his formidable speed and accuracy with a gun; but he hadn't gotten off a single shot at his slayer.

September 28th: John Henry Jackson, 33, a one-time paid spokesman for the Los Angeles chapter of the National Rifle Association, recently unemployed, but a law-abiding gun owner (at least until the night of his demise) was left in a clump of bushes near the ivy-draped tunnel to Hollywood

Dell. Investigators had surmised he'd been expecting to sell the semi-automatic weapons that were found in his unopened trunk.

Jackson had clearly been on his guard: The medical examiner was forced to pry Jackson's AR-15 from his cold, dead fingers. All indications were that his assailant jumped on him from the top of the overpass—the only shots he got off went wild, four slugs sprayed into the ceiling of the tunnel.

September 29th: Investigators theorized that the killer had gone underground when no victim was found on the morning of the thirtieth. Alas, this optimism was premature: The partially decomposed remains of Dade Cummings, 61, were located on October 2nd when a hiker's dog sniffed them out just inside the locked gate to Cummings' compound in Tujunga. An uncashed army pension check indicated he had picked up his mail from his postal box no earlier than September 29th, and the coroner fixed his time of death as sometime that night.

Cummings had been living off the grid for seven years: He had a cistern for water, an underground gasoline tank, and a generator for power; a quarter-century's worth of freeze-dried food; a jumbo-sized septic tank (this guy was *prepared*); and he was armed to the teeth with thousands of rounds of ammunition, ready for societal collapse and/or a zombie apocalypse. What he was not prepared for was the approach of whoever ripped through his spinal cord from behind.

One other thing struck Lisa: Though several attacks had occurred within two miles of other jurisdictions, including

Beverly Hills, Universal City, and Glendale, every one of these grisly killings was committed within the city limits of Los Angeles...and within two miles of Griffith Park.

Until Dade Cummings.

His compound backed into the hills above La Tuna Canyon, in the Sunland-Tujunga neighborhood at the northeastern edge of Los Angeles, some eighteen miles as the car crawls from Hollywood.

Why, Lisa, pondered, would even an insane thrill-killer go so far afield from his usual hunting grounds and single out the owner of the biggest arsenal of any of these well-armed victims?

The more she ran it all over in her mind, the less sense it made. Unless this killer had a serious death wish. Or some weird religious motive.

"You're even prettier than your pic," said a deep voice right above her.

Way above her. The guy was six-nine, if he was an inch. And a solid build. Maybe two hundred sixty pounds.

He could pose for the cover of Drake's book, thought Lisa, casually closing her laptop lid.

"You're Sally, right?"

She rose—which still only took her up to his sternum—and put out her hand.

"Sally Lowe. And you must be Edwin, uh...?"

"Jarrett." His hand was more like a bald paw; hers disappeared within it, but he held it gingerly, as if he'd picked up a freshly-laid egg.

"I guess I'm a little late. Sorry," he said, sitting down. "I see you finished your coffee."

"I could use another."

He stood up with startling speed, looking eight feet tall again. "Your wish is my command!"

"Thank you, Edmund."

He gave her an odd look.

"Edwin," she said with an embarrassed laugh. "Sorry. I used to know an Edmund. He was really tall like you."

"Not a problem," he said with a wry smile. "And it's... Cindy, right?"

Lisa gave a wry grin.

"Sally. Guess I deserve that."

"Oh, no. That's nothing like what you deserve." There was an awkward beat, then he swept his hand archly at the price board. "The sky's the limit. I just got paid. What'll you have?"

"Um...the Antarctic Java sounds good, thanks."

Edwin returned with their drinks.

Lisa took a sip. "So...tell me about yourself, Moonchild."

He winced and shook his head. "Oh, God. I knew that was a dumb profile name."

"Not at all. It made you stand out from the crowd."

He cast his eyes down. "Not that that's ever an issue for me."

"There's nothing wrong with Moonchild. It just means you were born in July, or late June. Right?"

Edwin gave a mirthless smile. "Yeah, dear old Mom was a nut for astrology...but she was terrified of cancer. So I was a moonchild."

"You say she *was*? So she passed away?"

"She died. No passing. Just died, like that." He snapped his long fingers loud—every customer in the place would have turned, except it was just the two of them.

He took a long pause and stared off, his voice flat. "It happened while I was at school. Her gardener found her at the bottom of the staircase. Broken neck."

"Oh, God. I'm so sorry, Ed."

He nodded but still didn't look her in the eye.

"Yeah. Did you know that's the most likely cause of death in the home, a fall? And stairs are the most dangerous place. Even worse than the bathroom."

There was another pause, so long you could drive a semi through it.

Lisa gave him a sunny smile and leaned forward. "Well, tell me about yourself. What do you do?"

"I don't really work if that's what you mean. Mom had life insurance. And I'm not really much for jobs anyway. So I spend a lot time doing research."

"Oh! Like what?"

"Just stuff. You know. Like...the most likely way to die in your home."

Lisa waited.

He finally gave a shy smile. "Just kidding."

Lisa forced a smile. "You have a quirky sense of humor, Ed. So, what do you like to do for fun?"

"I know what you like to do for fun. Ask a lot of questions."

"How else do you get to know someone?"

"Or is it for your job?"

"I told you, I'm a feature writer. Magazine articles."

"Are you researching me? 'My Ten Blind Dates'?"

"No, Ed. That's—"

"Edwin. My name is Edwin."

"Oh, sorry."

"I don't like 'Ed.'"

"Okay."

"Or Edmund. Sounds too much like Ed Kemper."

"Who?"

He looked around. The place was empty. The barista was at the rear, restocking.

"You and I both know this isn't going to result in a love connection," he said quietly. "So, let's just end this."

"Did I say something to upset you?"

"You *wore* something to upset me. Deliberately. I bet you don't dress like that for work. No, you wear a business jacket and a starched blouse and cover yourself up real well. But when you meet a guy like me on your own time, you dress to tease. That little tank top that shows everything you've got. A night like this, I bet when you step outside that cold air makes your nips stand right up."

Lisa clenched her jaw. "You're right. This *was* a mistake." She zipped up her laptop bag.

Edwin rose. "No, finish your drink. I'm leaving. Wouldn't want to inflict myself on such a lovely lady," he said softly, but the words dripped with contempt.

He walked out. She heard a van start up, and he pulled out of the tiny parking lot.

She waited a minute, taking a few calming breaths, then opened her laptop. Her fingers were still a little shaky, but she wanted to get down her notes about Edwin Jarrett immediately.

Her supposed slip of calling him "Edmund" was playing a long shot, but it just paid off. That he knew who Ed Kemper was and had lost his temper over it certainly wasn't proof any court would accept, but as far as she was concerned, Moonchild fit the profile. She tried to Google "Edwin Jarrett" but the little coffee shop had no wifi. Even the cell service was spotty here.

Lisa chucked her cup in the trash and headed out onto the avenue. At the corner, she hoofed it north up the tiny hillside street where she'd managed to find parking.

The big silver moon was now above the eastern hills.

Reaching her car, she let out a growl of exasperation—

some slob had thoughtfully set a beer bottle right at the curb, by her rear tire. Good thing she'd spotted it before pulling out of the space.

She crouched to remove it...and it was then she felt a sharp pain and everything went black.

4

THE FULL MOON KILLER

THE DRIVE WAS AS SILENT AS DINNER HAD been. Drake tried a new subject. Well, new to the car.

"You were right, that restaurant was awesome."

Nicole nodded, but remained lost in thought.

He forged ahead, "I'm glad you live so close to Thai Town."

More silence.

"Though I often wonder why they call it Thai Town. I mainly see yups with Bluetooths. Maybe they should call it Studio Intern Town."

"Or Unemployed Teacher Town."

Well, here it was. No avoiding the conversation that Drake had been steeling himself for all evening.

He pulled into a miraculously unoccupied section of curb in front of the Ridgeview Apartments, a sprawl of concrete and stucco backed up against the bone-dry brush of the Hollywood Hills. Remarkable for a Tinseltown location, this name was accurate—there was a view of the sparkling city lights from the rise behind the complex.

Drake undid his seatbelt and turned to her, earnest. "Nicole, I'm not going to be unemployed. Yeah, it sucks if I can't teach at the same place as you anymore, but I can still sub at other schools."

"If Dr. Benson makes enough trouble with the district, you won't be able to sub at *reform* school."

"They still have those?" Drake jutted out his lower jaw, as if it held an invisible toothpick and imitated a Dead End Kid: "Eh, Foddah, whadaya heah, whadaya say? When's Rocky gettin' outta da jernt?"

Nicole's expression said she would not be amused out of this discussion. "Drake, what happens when we start a family?"

"We'll have smart, beautiful kids, thanks to you. Who are a little weird and love scary stories."

"When I give birth, I won't be able to work."

"You won't have to. By then I won't be an unemployed substitute. I'll be a published author. I'm signing the book contract next week."

"They told you that last week. And the week before. And the month before that."

"It's just agent-lawyer-stuff. It's finally happening, Nicole. No more pitches, no more vanity presses. A real book contract with trade ads and author tours and an advance check we can blow on a honeymoon! You just need to have faith in me."

Nicole brought up her left hand—the small sapphire in her engagement ring glinted in the streetlamp light. At least, he was pretty sure he saw it. She laid that hand tenderly along his cheek. "Oh, Drake, I have *so much* faith in you. I always have, and I always will. You're the most brilliant guy I know." She looked at him, helpless, loving. She knew what that did to him.

He kissed her.

She kissed back.

He kissed back, back.

She kissed back, back, back.

And so on, until they lost count of the backs. It was a cold night, and the windshield was starting to steam up.

Finally, Nicole came up for air. "Um, speaking of faith..."

Drake kept nuzzling her earlobe and the nape of that lovely neck. He wanted her so bad he couldn't think straight. He breathed into her ear. "Babe, we're getting married a week from Sunday. I will not leave you at the altar. Do ten days really, really matter that much?"

She turned and looked at him with those big brown eyes. "Darling, I saved myself for you all my life. Can't you last another ten days?"

No, he thought. *This will kill me. My crotch will literally explode.*

But what he said was: "Of course I can. It's just another week and a half. A third of a month." He gave her his patented grin.

But Nicole detected the disappointment. She gave him another kiss. "You are the most patient, devoted, darling, loving, understanding man any woman ever had, and I'm the luckiest girl in the world."

Drake nodded. "Yes, you are."

No, you're not, he thought to himself.

He was the lucky one. Nicole might have been the only twenty-three-year-old virgin left in Los Angeles...almost certainly the only one who looked as delectable as Nicole did...but he knew he would love her till the day he died, and to spend the rest of his life with her, he would endure any kind of hell.

"I'll call you tomorrow. I love you," she said. She gave

him another kiss. An epic kiss. After a while, he tried to talk around her tenderly moving lips.

"Okay...c'mon...that's enough...Nicole. Have a heart. If you want me to wait ten days."

Nicole pulled back, a bit embarrassed. "I don't know what got into me." She lifted her eyes to the ridgeline, and her eyes lit up, reflecting the bright orb that rose above it. "Must be the moon."

She opened the passenger door. "Walk me to the lobby?"

Drake looked at the elderly couple dawdling at the lobby door, then at his lap. "That would be awkward. I'm not sure I can even get out from behind the steering wheel."

Nicole gave a fond chuckle.

"Poor Drake. It'll be worth it, I promise." Then she remembered. "And don't forget, we meet Kevin at the church, Thursday at noon.

"Well, thanks for mentioning your brother. Now I can turn the steering wheel."

Nicole giggled.

A police cruiser pulled over just ahead of Drake's car. Drake automatically buckled his seatbelt.

Nicole started to slide out, but he held onto her hand and pulled her back for just one more kiss. She smiled, and freed her hand.

"Come on, Drake. You act like this is the last time you'll ever see me."

The beast opened its eyes. Wakened in the silvery nighttime, it was ravenous. It loped silently down a trail redolent with the spoor of humans and their dogs. But near the base of the hill, an unbearable, poisonous reek made it halt and veer off its path. Then beyond a thicket, it heard movement. The scent of prey flooded its nostrils.

Nicole closed the car door. For a second, she thought she glimpsed motion in the bushes by the trail, but now there was nothing.

The elderly man in the lobby opened the front door for her as she headed inside.

Drake double-checked his seatbelt, looked in all three mirrors, engaged his turn indicator, looked over his shoulder, then carefully and safely pulled out into the travel lane. As he slowly passed the officer in the cruiser, their eyes met. Then the cop resumed his vigil. He seemed to be scanning the neighborhood, as if he expected trouble. Drake felt oddly comforted to see the city providing extra protection in this area. He'd heard the news stories.

Drake drove an extra three blocks up Beachwood before doing his illegal U-turn and heading back downhill.

The Beast peered through the limbs of the bush. Hunger gnawed. More sounds. The aroma of ripe young flesh. Prey showed itself.

The lobby door clicked shut behind Nicole. Now wearing Nikes and jogging clothes, her music plugged into her ears, she stopped to stretch her leg muscles. She sang along with the music as she pressed her hands against the rough, fluted concrete of the Beaux Arts streetlamp.

A dark shape suddenly rose up behind her. She saw the shadow and whirled.

"Oh, my God!" gasped Nicole. She yanked out her earbuds, spilling Katrina and the Waves into the cool night air. "You scared the life out of me!"

The burly LAPD officer with a buzz-cut and a nameplate that read "P. REYES" looked her over.

"Sorry, ma'am. But anybody could've walked up behind you and you wouldn't have heard, with those buds in."

Nicole nodded, guiltily. He had a point. She'd lived in this town long enough to know better.

"You're right," she panted.

"Especially a night like this. Don't you watch the news? You shouldn't be out walking alone."

Nicole caught her breath, finally.

"Thank you, officer. You're really sweet to warn me. But I'm not alone." She touched her gold crucifix. "And I won't be walking. Or even running slow, not after the adrenaline jolt *you* just gave me."

She patted the policeman's shoulder reassuringly. "Just let 'em try and catch me."

Then she stuck her earbuds back in and dashed off at an admirable clip, along the flagstone path through a decorative planting of blue flowers, and up the dirt trail beyond.

Officer Reyes watched her go, shaking his head.

"Walking on Sunshine," he muttered. Well, he'd tried. He turned back to his car.

That was when a huge dark shape he never fully saw leapt onto him, knocking him to the ground. Sharp teeth tore away his left shoulder.

Reyes screamed and with this right hand, managed to

26

draw his pistol, but before he could aim, jaws sank into his forearm, rending flesh and bone. Blood spouted. Then he couldn't feel the trigger, or his hand anymore. They simply weren't there.

Agony was all he felt as he was dragged into the chaparral where his world ended in darkness.

5

MOONCHILD

THE VEHICLE LURCHED TO A HALT, WAKING Lisa. She was on her back; her neck and her head were killing her. Her jaw was numb and for some reason she could only breathe through her nose. First, she smelled bleach, then dimly she made out the shape of the plastic jug. Near it lay a shovel. She blinked in the stygian darkness, until she could make out the dim interior of...a van? What the hell?

Now she remembered—someone had hit her on the back of the head, with what felt like a bat or a two-by-four. She wanted to rub the soreness, but she couldn't.

Adrenaline shot through her veins as she realized her wrists were tied together behind her, and her ankles were also bound—with plastic zip ties. Her jaw was numb because of a tight gag tied in her mouth. She was now fully awake, heart jackhammering in her chest. She had to—

The back door flew open and a huge shape stood over her, black against the moon. Edwin's big meaty hand grabbed her ankles and dragged her out of the van like a sack of laundry.

She gave a muffled cry as the back of her head hit the bumper, doubling her pain.

"Oh, sorry," he said and, absurdly, he seemed to mean it.

Through the tree branches, she glimpsed part of the Hollywood Sign. She was in Griffith Park. Likely she had been out only a few minutes.

Edwin put his hand behind her neck and gently lifted her to her feet. The full moon was still behind him, and she couldn't make out his features. He spoke in a low, calm tone.

"I know that gag is uncomfortable, but if I'm going to take it off, you have to promise me you won't scream."

Lisa nodded urgently.

"I mean it, Sally. One scream, and it's your last," he said. Steel flashed in the moonlight as he opened a huge buck knife.

Lisa nodded again. The cloth was literally gagging her, but she had to suppress the urge to vomit or she'd aspirate on it and choke to death.

Edwin poked her cheek with the knife point—then with a flick, sliced the gag away. Lisa spat it out and sucked in air.

"Edwin, please don't do this," she whispered, trembling.

"Sh," he said, with a finger to his lips.

He picked her up with one hand and tucked her under his arm, carrying her over to a patch of dry grass.

"Listen to me, please. I'm a police officer."

He snorted in derision.

She kept talking. "You haven't done anything yet that would get you the death penalty!"

He chuckled. "Says you. Anyway, I'm not worried about that. Our friend Edmund Kemper got the death penalty four decades ago. Ten victims. But he's still enjoying air conditioning, three squares a day, and all the TV he can stand."

"You're not going to get away with this. You kill a police officer and the entire LAPD will be after your ass."

"Yeah? Where's your backup? Where's the guys in the van listening to you on a wire."

"This wasn't a surveillance. I met you on my own time."

"You're a really bad liar, Sally."

"My name's not Sally. It's Lisa Chen. You can check my purse. Or did you drop that where you kidnapped me?"

Edwin's smirk vanished. "No, I'm not a rank amateur, thank you."

He carried Lisa back to the van and yanked open the passenger side door. Her handbag was on the floorboard. Lisa struggled with all her strength, but he kept his enormous arm securely clamped around her as he laid the knife on the seat.

"Quit squirming," he growled. He stuck his hand in her bag and pulled out her badge and her gun. He gave her a disappointed look. "Okay, *Lisa*. You know, you have to announce that you're a cop, or it won't stand up in court. And you told me you were a magazine writer," he said with exaggerated dismay.

"Give yourself up and I promise we'll go easy on you!" she said.

He tossed the badge and the gun back in the van.

"Swear to God, Edwin. You can just plead temporary insanity."

"Lower your voice," he murmured through clenched teeth. "A woman talking out loud is just the same to me as her screaming." He pushed the knifepoint an inch from her eye. "So pretend we're at the library." Edwin quietly shut the van door and carried her back to the dry grass.

She dropped her voice to a whisper. "Think this

through, Edwin. We were seen together at the coffee spot. We're on their security camera."

"If they had one, which they don't. See, dear old Mom owned that sweet little coffee place. Now it belongs to me. That's why I suggested it. And I don't have cameras or wifi or any of that shit."

"What about your barista?"

"Mercedes?" he snickered. "Nah. Poor kid's a total frybrain. It's part of her bohemian charm. In a day or two, she won't even be able to recall if her boss was there on the night in question, much less that you were."

"I paid with my credit card," said Lisa. "They'll trace it."

"Nope, you paid cash."

Lisa stared at him.

"Oh, yes, I was watching you from outside. Like I said, I'm no idiot."

"They'll find my car."

"I really doubt it. It's a Jap ride of just the right vintage, very popular target for theft, especially in my neighborhood. I left your windows down and the keys on the seat. It's a pretty safe bet that it's been swiped already. No doubt on its way to the chop shop. So all that leaves, cutie, is you."

Lisa felt a chill down her spine, like someone was walking on her grave. And Edwin probably was. With those giant hiking boots. This psycho had it all thought out. She flashed on the interior of the van—the shovel and the jug of bleach.

He dumped her on her back on the grass. She couldn't help the pained grunt, but she fixed him with a defiant look.

"Am I even your first victim?"

"Ha! You really are a cop," he chuckled. "To the end." He bent down with the knife. "All you just did is up the ante."

She tried not to look at the blade. "You're not going to kill me before you screw me, are you?"

"You should thank me for sparing you the grief."

"You don't think much of yourself, do you, Edwin?" she said with as much sympathy as she could muster.

He stopped, frowning down at her.

"You're going to kill me anyway. But how do you know you won't like sex with a real live girl? Try it. I guarantee you'll like it. I bet you'll even make *me* like it."

He shrugged, amused. "Hell, why not?" He looked at her jeans, trying to figure the logistics.

"Just slide them off."

The plastic around her ankles was in the way. He knelt beside her. The blade gleamed blue against the blackness of the night as he slit the zip tie.

At that instant, a distant, high howl cut through the night.

A wolf.

Edwin instinctively glanced to the west. Lisa kicked him in the balls with all her might.

Edwin sucked in air, and fell to his knees. The pain was so sharp he could only groan. Lisa leapt to her feet and kicked him on the side of his face. She staggered, almost losing her balance, then spun around.

"Hee-YAH!" she cried, delivering her most focused kick yet. Edwin sprawled on his back, moaning in pain.

Lisa could have run, but instead she dropped to the ground and began wriggling her ass over her bound hands. If she could get her hands in front of her, she might have a chance.

But he still gripped the knife, and the ache in his testicles was already cresting. He got to his feet. "Oho, you bitch," he chuckled as he spat out blood. "I *was* going to make this fast. But not now."

With one last yank, she got her bound hands over her butt, past her ankles, and out in front of her. Before he could reach her, she leapt to her feet and spun around.

"HA!" she kicked his face again. The bruises were starting to swell, and blood now flowed from his cut lip.

He lunged with the blade.

She clumsily blocked it with her tied hands.

The knifepoint poked her wrist, and a thin stream of blood began to trickle down her palms. He lunged again, and this time she brought her wrists up toward the blade—slitting the plastic tie. Her hands were free!

Lisa spun again as the blade slid past her top, and with a cry—"HA!" she kicked the back of his skull. He was on the ground, but he rolled away before her next kick could land and leapt to his feet.

She took off running, screaming for help.

She got less than ten yards before she felt his huge hand seize her shoulder. In an instant, she stopped, grabbed and twisted his arm—using his considerable momentum to toss him over her shoulder. He landed on an exposed rock, expelling a moan, and the knife skittered from his hands, lost in the dark. But the throw only made him mad—well, madder.

With a roar, Edwin jumped up, fists knotted, itching to batter her bloody.

His first punch missed and she caught his second and delivered a hard neck chop that made him yelp. He swung and missed again.

"HA!" Another neck chop! One more punch that she blocked and trapped, then she delivered a kick to his chest —"HA!" She felt his rib crack.

"FUUUUCK!" he screamed in fury. He seized her neck and lifted her off the ground—then she slammed her palms hard against his ears.

He yelped and dropped her. But the pain from his ruptured eardrums might as well have been rocket fuel—he again launched himself at her with a feral roar.

Lisa delivered a spinning sidekick that ought to have broken his arm. She'd gotten her black belt at sixteen, and not at any McDojo. She'd snapped inch-thick boards with her hands and feet. But they hadn't been wrapped in the kind of muscle that covered Edwin's bones.

He paused, breathing hard. She'd lost the element of surprise—now he knew what she was capable of. He also knew he had the reach and the power to take her out. He just had to avoid those lethal feet of hers.

He forced her back. She could feel the breeze of punches that barely missed her. She knew if he landed even one blow with his huge fist, she'd be out cold...and dead soon after.

She kept an eye on his knees, hoping for a quick end to this, but he was playing it cagey now, and she couldn't get in close enough. She needed to make him reckless.

"Come on, you wimp," she taunted. "Can't you even take a punch from a girl?"

He dove at her in a fury, but she got under his outstretched hands and snapped a kick at his knee. He screamed in pain and collapsed. She punched his throat, then delivered a roundhouse kick to the back of his head.

Edwin kissed the ground and lay motionless, one hand pinned beneath him.

Lisa waited, ready to finish him off.

"Get up!" she commanded.

"Can't," he gurgled. "Can't breathe! I give up."

Good, she thought. How do I call for backup?

The van was twenty yards away. Her phone should still be in her bag. "Don't move."

"Can't breathe!" he repeated in a whisper. "Please, help me!"

Shit, I must have collapsed his windpipe, she thought. "Okay, take it easy."

He was on his face. She nudged his shoulder, but he didn't respond. She bent to turn him over.

In his right hand was a rock—she only saw it at the last instant.

He might have brained her with it, but the brutal beating had slowed him just enough that he only grazed her eyebrow. She staggered back, feeling only the shock, not yet the pain of it. Then a warm trickle of blood ran into her eye socket.

"Goddamn it!" she yelled and stomped the hand that held the rock.

Jarrett shrieked, then he lunged once more, teeth bared to tear a chunk out of her thigh. He missed. A second later, she kicked his teeth out.

6

SCENARIOS

LIEUTENANT MARC GUTIERREZ HAD A POUCHY, lived-in face that belied his sharp interrogation style. As they sat in an otherwise empty lounge at Good Samaritan Hospital, he flipped through the report.

Lisa knew the drill—he needed all the information she'd already told the responding officers, and what she told him now had better match what she'd told them to a T.

"It doesn't look good, right now. Edwin Jarrett doesn't have a rap sheet. He had one parking ticket in the last five years, and he paid it on time."

"Maybe he had something as a juvenile. Fights, animal cruelty...I mean, I know those records are sealed. But..."

"The point is, detective, Jarrett was not a known offender when you encountered him. But according to you, he assaulted you, kidnapped you, and attempted to rape and murder you."

Lisa nodded. Gutierrez consulted the hospital's printout.

"So. In addition to giving him a concussion, a black eye, numerous contusions, lacerations, and soft-tissue injuries, you broke your suspect's kneecap, his left tibia, his right arm, and four of his fingers."

"Well, I was fighting for my life, sir."

"He's also missing four incisors."

"He tried to bite me."

Gutierrez closed the reports and slid back in the chair. He looked up at the ceiling.

"Detective, there are two scenarios here. By the time that waste of skin wakes up tomorrow, our forensic team will have gone over his property with the proverbial fine-tooth comb for any trace of other victims. You'd better hope they find at least one. Because in scenario one, they find some souvenir, or bit of DNA that we can tie to a missing person or a Jane Doe homicide; in that scenario, you were simply a lonely woman who, in her spare time, created a fictional profile for a coffee date because guys act weird when they know a girl's a cop. You were not on the clock. And you definitely did not have a strategy."

"Lieutenant, that's not the truth. I developed a theory that a serial killer like Full Moon would have to be on social media to find a specialized set of victims. So I—"

Gutierrez cut her off. "You were not in any way surveilling a dating website. You were looking for romance. And that's how you accidentally stumbled across this serial killer who nearly murdered you."

"But—"

"In scenario one, you will be a hero for beating the living shit out of a murderous monster and getting him off the street. You will be in line for a commendation. Probably on the fast track to sergeant. That's the way we all hope this goes. Right?"

His eyes bored into her. Lisa didn't say no. "Scenario two

is if the lab boys find nothing. Which would then indicate that you would have been Jarrett's first victim. In that event, an aspiring homicidal psychopath will go scot-free. And he will have you to thank, because this comic book vigilante act of yours will have irrevocably tainted our case against him."

"Lieutenant..." began Lisa.

"The city will no doubt wind up settling out of court with him. If we're lucky, for only seven figures. In that event, you will not get a commendation, and you will not be on any kind of track to sergeant, or for that matter, to meter maid. Your career with this department will be over." He regarded her somberly. "Have I made myself clear about how the two scenarios work?"

"Yes, sir. May I go home now? I'm working the day watch tomorrow."

"And if I know you, you'll be at work an hour early. No, Detective Chen. You're going to stay here and get a CAT scan and anything else the docs ask you for. I want every scratch, bruise, and 'owie' treated and listed on your chart. The more injuries you have, the better for you, if you take my meaning."

Lisa touched the dressing over her eye, and showed him the other on the back of her wrist.

"Seriously? That's it?" sighed Gutierrez. "Well, take some selfies."

"I also have quite a knot at the base of my skull. But I was only out for a couple minutes. I just need a little sleep."

"Do the scan. Then go home and get some shut-eye. And no more of this Nancy Drew crap. If you have any other brilliant theories, you run them by your boss, Lieutenant James. Got it?"

Lisa nodded and rose to leave, but then she paused.

"Lieutenant, you seem convinced that Jarrett isn't the Full Moon Killer. May I ask why?"

"You may. Because at the same time as you were having your little cage match with Jarrett, the real Full Moon Killer was ripping apart one of our officers up on Beachwood Canyon."

7

NEED TO KNOW

K NUCKLES RAPPED SHARPLY ON DRAKE'S DOOR, with an insistence that said pretending he wasn't home was not an option.

"LAPD! Open up!"

Drake shook off the dream. He didn't remember it, but it was definitely about Nicole because it had left him frustratingly aroused.

The knuckles banged harder. Drake pressed the heels of his hands against his eyeballs then forced binocular vision to align on the digital clock. He swore at what he saw.

Now it was the side of a fist rattling the whole doorframe, making it clear the next move would be to kick the door down. He knew that could and would happen. So his feet hit the frigid oak floorboards, and he cursed under his breath. He was wearing only boxers, and he'd left his ratty terrycloth bathrobe hanging by the door.

"It's not even seven A.M.!" he croaked. "Go screw yourself!"

"Guess you'd be the expert on *that*," said the detective as Drake yanked open the door.

Drake's eyes were downcast to avoid the first blinding rays of dawn. They focused on the gold shield defiantly pinned to a leather belt. Then his blurry vision tilted up the crisp purple blouse and dark jacket to a fall of black hair framing the deadpan face of Lisa Chen. Like it could have been anyone else with that voice.

She gave him the once-over, then broke into a grin as he hurriedly knotted the belt of the robe. "Cheer up, Drake. Just nine more days till your honeymoon."

He debated slamming the door again, but she had a cup of Peet's steaming in each hand, and the aroma wafting from under the plastic lids told him the contents would make the difference between immediate wakefulness and daylong catatonia.

Drake opted for the former.

He stood aside, hand sweeping wide in courtly invitation, and Lisa breezed in, handing him his cup. He shut the door.

"Thanks for the coffee and sympathy."

"No sweat. How's Nicole holding out?"

"You mean, holding up?"

"Sure, that's what I meant," she said dryly.

He let that one pass as she scanned his room. He quietly peeled back the lid.

Without turning back, Lisa said, "I already put in the milk. No sugar. Right?"

Of course right.

Then she turned her head, and her hair flowed to one side, revealing a bandage just above her eyebrow.

"What's this?" he said, pointing.

"None of your business."

Drake shrugged. "Well, speaking of my business, if you'll

excuse me..." He left the cup on the counter and went in the bathroom.

Lisa continued her inspection of Drake's rented guesthouse: Probably an artist's studio at one time, now a studio apartment with a built-in dresser/closet, small but experienced couch, dinette-for-two, office chair, cramped three-quarters bath, kitchenette with sink, mini-fridge, microwave and toaster oven, plus that antique hall tree Drake had found at the Rose Bowl swap meet...and speaking of antiques, a Panasonic answering machine...all battling with the bed for elbow room in two hundred square feet.

Nevertheless, it was trimmed in classic oak from the floorboards to the ceiling molding. Pretty nice work, too—what you could see of it. Lisa noticed it was fuller than when Drake had first moved in. Every wall was either an actual bookcase, or one improvised from planks and cinderblocks, all bursting with books—hardbound, paperback, notebooks, comic books—standing up, on their sides, books wedged atop other books. Antiques. Didn't this guy own a Kindle?

And everywhere, those yellow legal pads Drake loved to scribble his first drafts in.

What little wall space remained was covered in posters and prints and maps, some crusty, musty artifacts and, amusingly, Drake's accordion, which she was pretty sure he hadn't played since high school.

Drake came out of the bathroom.

Lisa looked around and gave a low whistle. "Dang, did this place get smaller?"

"I brought in more books. I do a lot of research." He took a sip of the joe. Just right.

"I know you do. That's why I'm here."

He squinted at the Band-Aid on her forehead. "Seriously, what's with this?"

"I'll tell you sometime, when I think it won't make you faint."

"Cut yourself shaving, maybe?"

"Are you always this droll first thing in the morning?"

"What do you want, Lisa?"

"To throw some paid work your way. Consulting on a case. I mean, if you're not too busy with your big book tour."

"What's this, your idea of charity?"

"No, seriously. I remember all those times you talked my ear off about Satanic rituals, Black Masses and all that. Well, now I'm on a case that sounds like we're dealing with that, and I can't find anyone else who knows this crap the way you do."

"Look, this is really sweet, but I'm pretty busy already. In fact, I have this book signing at Broman's, so..."

"Really? Can I come?"

"You're welcome to come, Leese, but it's not till tonight."

"Oh, good! So you're free this morning."

Damn her! He'd walked right into another of her little verbal traps. "You just love to trip me up, don't you? You know, this is why you can't keep a partner."

Lisa frowned. He couldn't have hurt her feelings, could he? "Drake, it's a homicide," Lisa admitted. "A cop. I knew him, a little. Pete Reyes. Saw him a lot at the gun range. He was found a couple hours ago, up by Ridgeview Apartments."

"Ridgeview? That's Nicole's building!" Drake ran to his bed and grabbed his cell phone. Lisa put a hand on his arm.

"Don't worry, Nicole's in no danger. I checked the window of her unit. She's fast asleep and there's no need to wake her."

Drake was both relieved and a little creeped out that Lisa had done this. He yanked on socks and jammed his legs into his jeans. "What was it, a shooting?"

"No. If it were, I wouldn't need you."

"Then what?"

"I'd rather you tell me after you see him."

He tossed the robe onto the brass hook and wriggled into yesterday's half-buttoned shirt.

"Why didn't you tell me where it was, right off?"

"Because I'm telling you now."

Drake stopped buttoning, and stared at her. "You just *had* to see if I would act guilty, didn't you?"

"No, that wasn't it," said Lisa.

Drake was skeptical. "You know that I drop her off there. So you couldn't resist pulling your detective act on me."

"Drake, I've known you since kindergarten. As your friend, I'm sure you'd never kill anyone. But as an investigator on this case, I give out information on a need-to-know basis."

Drake jammed a black running shoe on his right foot and knotted it hastily. "Well, since you've asked for my help, I'd say I need to know. Wouldn't you? So when were you planning to tell me where this happened? When we pulled up in front of my fiancée's apartment house?"

"Around then, yeah. I was going to ask you *when* you dropped Nicole off last night...and if you noticed anything unusual."

Drake had put on another shoe and had it tied before he realized it was gray. He cursed under his breath but kept it on. "We had dinner early. It was just getting dark when I dropped her. Maybe 6:30, or a little later?" Then he remembered. "Wait a sec. I passed a cop parked out front in his car.

He looked like he was on a stakeout. Was that the officer who...?"

Lisa nodded. "Pete Reyes."

Drake finished knotting the lace. "What time was he killed?"

"He last called in at 6:46 P.M. The coroner's preliminary estimate is, he died about twelve hours ago, which means not long after you saw him."

"Oh, my God. Nicole usually goes for a run in the evening! She could have just missed the killer!"

Lisa pondered that. "Yeah. Looks like we will need to wake her."

"Oh, come on. You know damn well she'd have called the cops if she'd seen anything wrong."

"Actually, I don't know that."

"I'm going to assume you're being funny."

"I only mean, I don't really know Nicole that well. She was three years behind us. I'd *like* to know her better, but you haven't exactly..."

Drake snatched his corduroy jacket off a brass hook on the hall tree. "Let's just stick to discussing your homicide. I'll call Nicole and let her know we're coming." He snagged his keys and they hurried out.

8

IN THE BAG

T HE CORONER'S INVESTIGATOR UNZIPPED THE cadaver pouch. As many horror stories as Drake had written, he had not seen much of death close up and absolutely nothing to compare with the butchery inside that bag. He was instantly grateful he hadn't had breakfast.

Drake held up his hand—seven seconds was all he needed. The investigator zipped the bag up again, and Drake headed back to the building entrance.

Other neighbors, in various stages of dressing for work, were out on their patios rubbernecking.

Nicole was now at the door talking to Lisa. Nicole had thrown a jacket over her light dress and jumped into some Ugg boots. Lisa was holding Nicole's running shoes from last night in a clear plastic bag. Evidence, Drake assumed, as he hurried to the door.

Drake could see she was shivering when he arrived. "Babe, why are you out here? It's freezing."

Nicole indicated the trailhead, a hundred yards away. "I was just showing Lisa the spot where I was running last night when I met the officer." Tears welled up and her voice went shaky. "Oh, God, Drake, this is so awful. I *talked* to him. He told *me* to be careful."

Drake pulled her into a hug. "It's okay."

Lisa forged ahead. "So you didn't hear anything once you left him?"

"No. But I had my music cranked up."

"Which way did you run?"

"Up the flagstones to the trail that winds around the hill."

"Was the officer here when you returned?"

"I don't know. I didn't come back this way. I ran around the back of the hill, and the trail comes out on the, what is that...?" Nicole pointed down Beachwood.

"The south side?" said Lisa.

"Right, south side. And I came right back in the lobby door. I never looked over at where he was. I had no idea..."

Nicole misted up again, and Drake gave her a supportive squeeze. "So, is that all you need?" he asked Lisa.

"For now. But if you remember anything else, please call." Lisa handed Nicole her card.

Nicole looked skeptical, and her gaze flicked over to the balcony where the activity was watched by two neighbors.

"I called you guys a week ago, when Bluto over there hit his wife. Nobody came."

Lisa and Drake followed her gaze to a balcony overlooking the street and quickly recognized whom Nicole meant: a hefty guy in his thirties, gripping an aluminum can.

"Coors. There's a hearty breakfast," observed Drake.

Lisa peered at the man. He was wearing grubby work pants and a windbreaker over a sleeveless undershirt. Lisa shook her head. "God, he's actually *wearing* a wifebeater."

Hanging back behind him was a mousy dishwater

blonde in a bathrobe, with a purple bruise on her cheekbone.

Lisa turned back to Nicole. "Do you know their names?"

"Not his," said Nicole. "He's kinda scary. Her name is Alice. They're a few doors down, in 110."

Lisa tapped the info into her smartphone. "I'll pull their info later. And next time, call *me*. I'll come."

"Okay," nodded Nicole. She checked her watch. "Well, I need to get to work."

"I'll walk you back in," said Drake.

"No, no, I'm fine. You stay, help them solve this thing."

Nicole gave him a tender kiss then hurried back into her building.

Lisa led Drake up to the crime scene, cordoned off with yellow perimeter tape strung three feet off the ground. She leapt over the tape with a lithe kick. Drake was impressed—damn, at twenty-six, Lisa had lost none of her athletic grace. He thought about following suit, but the possibility of doing a faceplant in front of Lisa's cop buddies wasn't appealing. He raised the tape and ducked under it.

They approached the reddish-brown smear that began on the sidewalk and led right onto the dirt, which was dark where the blood had soaked in. The surrounding amber foxtail grass and the bushes were splattered a similar crimson hue.

Beside the stained concrete was a metal news rack facing the street. A splash of dried blood half-covered the plastic window. Inside lay an unsold copy of yesterday's *Los Angeles Times*, with the left-column feature headlined: "Police on Alert for Full Moon Killer." The subhead in smaller type: "9 Slain in Previous 3 Months."

Drake had been following the story. Another serial killer

on the loose, and this one was quite literally a lunatic. But it was one thing to read descriptions like "mutilated" and "cannibalized." It was quite another to see the gruesome results bagged in front of you. He found somewhere else to look as the transport crew wheeled the zipped-up body bag past him to their van.

Lisa indicated the news rack. "The *Times* vendor came to fill this up. Instead, he found Officer Reyes."

Drake nodded.

"Did you take a look at the body?" Lisa asked.

"Briefly." Drake shuddered at the memory.

"Need more time?"

"No!"

"You notice his right hand was...?"

"Yeah. Not there anymore. I saw."

"Okay. So, what do you think?"

Drake shook his head. He felt useless. "I don't see how I can help you, Leese. He was just...ripped to shreds. I've never..." Words failed him.

Lisa winced, regretful. "I know, and I'm sorry you had to see that."

Well, he didn't want her pitying him. "Hey, you know writers. Everything's research." Or else nightmare material, he didn't add. How did she do this job without screaming herself awake every morning?

"Can I ask...is this the work of that serial killer in the news?"

"We're not sure," Lisa admitted. "Last night was the first full moon of October, and so far no other victims have turned up. But this attack has certain...anomalies from the others."

"I don't know autopsy stuff," Drake began. "And all I

know about your case is what's in the papers. Maybe this is your Full Moon Killer. *Maybe* a human being could have done all that. But to me, it just looked like a wild animal tore into him."

"Trust me, the other bodies were just as bad. And they all happened on a full moon night. Always an isolated spot with no witnesses or security cams. All of the victims were well-armed and expert shots. But whoever attacked them was pretty damn fast, because not one of them managed to shoot their assailant before they died.

"Another weird thing is, we never find shoe prints. And there's no weapon used other than teeth, as far as we can tell. But as savage as they are, we have reason to suspect a human being did those killings."

"You have DNA evidence?"

"No. Not a drop of blood, or even a hair that doesn't match the victims."

"How is that possible?"

Lisa rolled her eyes. "You watch a lot of procedurals, don't you? Look, forget about everything you see on TV. I just want to know what you think of this scene. Take your time. But watch where you step."

Drake looked around. A scarlet paw print on the concrete was unmistakable. "One of your anomalies?"

She nodded.

"We haven't found these at the other attacks. That's why we thought this might have been an animal attack. Or, theory B, maybe a scavenger was attracted by the smell of blood *after* a homicide."

"That looks like a coyote track."

"That's what we thought, at first. But our wildlife expert says this is too big for a coyote. He says it has to be a wolf— and a huge one."

"Well, I'm no wildlife expert, but I do know there haven't been any wolves in Southern California since, like, maybe the Great Depression. Long before our time, anyway."

"So I'm told. But there's one here now. Some people keep wild animals illegally. We found these prints in the blood and in the dirt all over here, and they lead up into the brush, where they end. But you know what's weird? Every single one that we can find is a *rear* paw print."

"That is weird. Wolves don't walk upright."

"And we've found no shoeprints or human footprints, except Nicole's. It rained yesterday afternoon, and it seems she was the only human being on this dirt trail since them. Now, if it was only a wolf that was here, this would not be a murder. It'd be a case for Animal Control. But check this out."

Lisa led Drake up the flagstone pathway, with the blue floral beds on their left hand side and bushes beyond that, and behind the bushes a hiking trail that intersected the path at an angle some fifty yards farther on.

"Nicole started out here on the stone path, and from the tracks we found, the wolf was on the trail, over there beyond the flowerbed and all these bushes."

"Wait—are you saying this wolf could have been twenty feet away when *Nicole* was here?"

"Not 'could have been.' It definitely was."

"What?!"

By this time, they had reached the point where the flagstone path ended on a diagonal at the dirt trail. Lisa pointed to a shoeprint in the now-dry soil, with a noticeable crack in one tread.

"This is one of Nicole's. It matches her shoe. And it's partly on top of a paw print. That means she ran over the same ground after the wolf had stepped on it. And before it attacked our officer."

"Jesus! It could have attacked *her!*"

"Exactly. It was closer to Nicole, and she was smaller prey. So if this *was* a wolf attack...why not rush across this flower bed and attack? Why did it go out of its way to attack Reyes, fifty yards away down on the sidewalk, instead of her?"

Drake gave a shiver at the thought. "I know what Nicole would say: that God was watching out for her. Hell, I'm no zoologist. What I know is cults and folklore and black magic."

"That's why I asked you to come. Listen to this."

Lisa pulled out her phone and tapped it a few times. It played back a male voice that had been digitally scrambled. *"I didn't want to kill that policeman. But I saw the pentagram in his hand. You've got to stop me."*

Lisa ended the playback.

"This recording is another new wrinkle in the case. It came in to Lieutenant James' line around sunrise this morning. He's the lead investigator on the case. So I'm going on the theory that the wolf tracks are just a coincidence, and this homicide is our Full Moon Killer's work. Except now he's phoning us. It's like he wants to be caught. So what kind of human likes pentagrams and would leave a corpse like that? I mean, could we be talking Satanists?"

Drake kept looking at the cerulean-hued planting between the flagstone path and the trail as he mulled over a crazy hunch. He turned to Lisa. "No, I doubt it. The pentagram is a mystical symbol many cults have used. But there's no pentagrams, or any other ritual signs on the ground, like there'd be in a Black Mass. And Satanists don't kill with their teeth, as far as I ever heard. And for sacrifices, they favor out-of-the-way spots, not public sidewalks. However…"

Drake took two quick steps down the flagstone walk and picked one of the blue flowers. He returned, handing it to Lisa with a flourish. She cocked an eyebrow.

"Thanks, but, uh…aren't you engaged?"

"Yes, and that reminds me, how much am I getting paid for this consulting gig?"

"Depends. Tell me what this little blossom is."

"It's aconite. Also known as monkshood. Or more famously as wolfsbane."

"I thought the word was wolfbane."

"Most people call it that. It's easier to say."

"But you're saying this plant is something that wolves avoid?"

"Ask your wildlife guy about that. What I'm saying is that aconite was known to contain poison, and in medieval folklore, it was *believed* it would ward off wolves. Including werewolves. Now, Nicole ran past this flowerbed. But I don't think there was a real wolf here, on the far side of that bush. I'm willing to bet there was a human killer here who followed this dirt trail all the way down to the street to attack your officer…because he did not want to cross over these wolfbane flowers to get to Nicole."

It wasn't until after Drake heard himself say the words that he realized their import. It was sheer luck he didn't lose her last night!

"Look, I need to talk to Nicole." And he did need that, right away. To hold her.

He started back, but Lisa grabbed his arm.

"Wait, wait! Why the pentagram?"

Drake took out his pen, grabbed Lisa's hand, and quickly drew a five-sided star on her palm.

"*The Wolf Man*, 1941. Hollywood's second werewolf movie. Lon Chaney, Jr. would get a vision of the pentagram in the palm of his next victim."

Drake was now on a bearing toward the lobby, but Lisa was an anchor, slowing him.

"You're suggesting that we're dealing with the Wolf Man?"

Drake exhaled, impatient."Grow up. What I think you're dealing with is a lycanthrope. A psychotic serial killer who *thinks* he's a werewolf. So he avoids wolfbane. And takes his cues about werewolfery from old movies. Now, can I go?"

"This is great, Drake! But what about the paw prints?"

"Lycanthropes sometimes collect wolf pelts and other body parts. They believe it helps them transform. He probably had the paw with him while murdering your officer. If I were you, I'd check your crime scene photos of prior Full Moon Killings. I bet on those, you'll find paw prints that you overlooked."

Lisa tapped more info into her smartphone, but kept talking to him. "You've done your homework, I'll give you that. But I'm curious—I don't recall you ever writing a story about a werewolf, or a lycanthrope. Did I miss one?"

"Nope."

"Any reason why not?"

"Let's just say, I got off on the wrong paw with that topic."

Lisa looked up at him from her screen, puzzled.

Drake broke free of her grip and was already jogging backwards toward the lobby door. "Look, I need to check on Nicole. I'll send you some links."

Lisa called after him. "Okay. Thanks, Drake. You da monster man!"

He was almost to the door when she called out again. "Good luck at the signing!"

He waved without turning back and went inside.

Lisa sniffed the wolfbane flower, and a funny smile came to her lips.

9

THE DEAN OF HORROR

S NAGGING A DIAGONAL SLOT IN FRONT OF **Broman's Books** meant circling the block, scanning eagle-eyed, until you glimpsed the telltale flicker of back-up lights that meant you had won the parking lottery. You must then immediately brake, far enough behind the occupant that he or she could back out without hitting you, yet not so far back that someone could swing around you and steal it, but also not so suddenly as to be rammed by the driver who'd been tailgating you at thirty miles an hour, determined to nab a spot himself.

This neighborhood, just south of Glendale, was called Atwater, but it belonged to the City of Los Angeles. L.A. remained a frontier town in a few ways, and it was not unheard of for a traffic dispute to be settled by gunplay. You could wind up expiring before your parking meter did.

In two hours, when it was dark, backing out onto a street that fed onto the Golden State Freeway would be an even dicier proposition, especially if, say, you'd had to park between a pair of hulking vans that formed a tunnel of zero peripheral vision.

There were, however, two spaces in the tiny lot behind the store. One bore the name of the owner, Mrs. B., and the other one was reserved for her very special guest.

———

The card on the table read "Meet Drake Callahan, 'The Monster Man'—Author Signing, 5 to 7 PM."

A long, long line of fans clutching books snaked toward the table where Drake sat with brand new paperback copies of *The Monster Man*, ready with a sturdy black ballpoint pen, plus half a dozen back-ups, and a green calligraphy pen, just for variety.

Unfortunately, the queue did not lead to Drake. It passed him, then went past a potted plant in an urn, a table of marked-down stationery items, a second potted plant, a premature display of Christmas books, yet another plant, and a card rack, finally arriving at a second table, which bore a different card:

"Meet Peter Zaar, the Dean of Horror Novelists, signing 'The Unalive'—3 to 5 PM."

Zaar, tall and rakishly handsome, had just breezed past forty-one, with the visible damage limited to the merest hint of distinguished silver in his jet-black hair and Van Dyke beard. Other than that, he still resembled his book jacket photo.

Zaar endorsed a hardbound copy for a bespectacled fanboy.

"Here you go, Justin," he smiled.

Justin took the book, but not the hint. "Peter, have you ever thought about revisiting the post-apocalyptic world you created for *Planetful of Corpses*?"

Barely angling his wrist, Zaar glanced at his Rolex. It was 4:58.

"If you check peterzaar.com, there'll be some news. I'm really sorry, but there's a long line and I need to leave on time."

Blushing, Justin moved along.

"Ouch. Want some ice for that burn?" smirked his friend, who'd been in line right behind him. However, the friend was less amused when he got a good look at his own book's endorsement, which was definitely a rush job.

Justin noticed and returned the smirk.

Then a hand tapped the fanboy's shoulder. He turned, and his jaw went slack as he beheld Nicole.

"Hi. It's Justin, right?"

"How'd you know my...?"

"I overheard you. Have you read *The Monster Man*?"

Justin suddenly remembered to swallow a large amount of saliva that he had built up in his mouth.

"Um, sorry. No. I thought I had all of Zaar's titles. Is that new?"

She pointed to Drake's table.

"It's by Drake Callahan. He's great. It's terrifying."

"Oh, I thought you meant..." Justin looked back at Zaar, now an autograph machine, scribbling in books as fast as they were proffered. Justin looked back at Nicole.

"I'm sure it's good and all. But you know, Zaar writes them so fast it's all I can do to keep up with *him*." He checked Nicole out, hopeful. "So what are you, like, this Drake guy's girlfriend?"

"Yes. We're engaged." Nicole flashed the ring with a sheepish smile.

Justin nodded glumly. Just as he'd suspected. He and his

pal gravitated back to a distant orbit around the master's table, hoping to hear something quotable.

Odetta Broman surveyed her store as she descended from the upper floor. She was in her mid-fifties, mocha-hued and freckled, not much more than five feet tall, and built for comfort, pillowy everywhere.

Through her oversized glasses, she observed with satisfaction that Peter Zaar's line had finally picked up the pace. It looked like he'd satisfy the demand for signed copies more or less on time. She placed a "Line Closed" stanchion behind the last fan in the queue. A late-arriving fan looked like he was going to question her decision, but Odetta cocked an eyebrow, and the guy elected not to push it.

Had he but known...Odetta was the biggest pushover in town. If he'd given her any kind of sob-story, she'd have let him in line.

Odetta noticed Drake talking to a tall, striking redhead and hoped this was a good sign. As she arrived, she heard the end of the transaction.

"It's just upstairs to the right."

The redhead nodded and ascended the staircase, empty-handed.

"How many have you sold?" asked Odetta.

"Well, if you buy one, one."

"Sold."

"Thanks, Mrs. B."

"Don't thank me, just sign it." She scanned the table. "Don't you have a hardcover?"

Drake pulled one out of his briefcase. "Just this one. I've been saving it for you."

"Are you crazy? One of your readers is going to want that. I'll wait till you get more. So, where *are* the rest?"

"I'm supposed to get them tonight. There was some screw-up with the delivery yesterday. I knew I wouldn't be home today, so I told them to redeliver *here*. They promised faithfully they'd be here by five."

"If they can find parking." She looked down at her vintage brooch watch. "It's almost five. Peter has to be leaving."

"That should free up a lot of parking spaces," Drake sighed.

Odetta gently pinched his cheek. "That's not what I mean, and you know it. I mean, you can catch his overflow."

Drake nodded. "I can try."

Odetta looked over at the crowd behind Zaar.

Nicole was working to peel off another disciple. She pointed to Drake and his pile of paperbacks. She was giving it her all, but it was no sale. From across the room, Nicole gave Drake an I-tried shrug.

He blew her a kiss.

Odetta shook her head. "You are one lucky boy, Drake. You best marry that girl soon."

"In nine days, Mrs. B. And if I could speed it up, I would."

Odetta guffawed. "I bet you would."

"You know, we did invite you. There's still plenty of room."

"And who's going to run my store? I'll be there in spirit, honey."

Zaar had nearly finished with his line. He was halfway out of his chair, his body language screaming, 'lemme outta here.'

Nicole hurried over to Drake. "Sweetie, you should say hi."

"No, I definitely should not."

"But Zaar's fans would love your stuff. And it couldn't hurt for them to see you and him chatting."

"Nicole, no."

She leaned in close, pressing against him, running her finger down his shirtfront. She usually got what she wanted when she did that. "Come on, give me one good reason why not."

"Because I'm not a fan of his work. Stephen King is ten times the writer Zaar is, and a great guy to boot."

"You used to be a big fan of them both. I remember."

"I remember, too."

Drake stepped up to the mic, and a spotlight hit him. He hadn't counted on that, and reflexively closed his lips, then angled his head down as he spoke, so the spotlight wouldn't glint off his braces.

"Um, huge fan, Mr. Zaar. I've read all your stories."

His hair fell into his eyes and he brushed it back over his ear.

Zaar nodded from his seat onstage. "Thanks. What's your question?"

"Well, I read your first story, 'Death By Silver'..."

"Wow, you are a fan. How did you find that one?"

"It was in an old copy of *Weird Tales* I found at a garage sale."

"The first one I ever sold."

"I know. Why didn't you ever anthologize it? I thought it was great!"

"I guess it had a certain juvenile charm."

"It had more than that. It was excellent. Amazing atmosphere. You really should republish it."

Zaar lifted an eyebrow, flattered. "Well, you've made me reconsider it. Perhaps I will."

Zaar grinned, and Drake grinned back at his literary hero. This was so cool…he'd made a connection. It was like he was in a bar discussing fiction with a chum. A *colleague*.

"I hope you will. And you could fix that little thing about the cop's bullet." An inside reference, just for those in the know. A wink between colleagues. But Zaar's face was a blank.

"Well, you already know that." Drake turned to hand the mic back to the assistant.

"Come again?"

The chill in Zaar's tone should have warned Drake off, but he was nineteen and not exactly cum laude in the Social I.Q. department, so when the assistant handed the mic back to Drake, he took it.

"WELL, IT'S JUST…"

The assistant pushed Drake's arm down, moving the mic from his mouth. "It's not an ice cream cone," she whispered.

He mouthed 'sorry' at her.

"It's just, when Jack drops his gun, then kills the first werewolf with the gun the cop dropped?"

Zaar looked around, with a mock frown. "You're supposed to say 'spoiler alert.'"

The audience laughed. Drake was, just slightly, starting to regret ever getting up with a question. "Oh, right. Well, that happens on page three, so I just thought it wasn't really…"

"What's your point?" Zaar was apparently smiling. But Drake saw it wasn't a smile.

"It...it's nothing."

"No, I'm intrigued now. How would you improve my story?"

A ripple of titters spread through the audience, as if a drop of blood had plopped into a shark tank.

This was turning into a nightmare. The last thing Drake wanted was to piss off one of his writing heroes. Who was now staring at him, requiring an answer.

"Well, since the cop didn't believe in werewolves, he wouldn't have had silver bullets in his gun. Right? I mean, it's an easy fix. Jack doesn't drop his gun."

Zaar paused, thinking back. He heard a murmur of laughter, this time at his expense. And somewhere out in the dark, in the cheap seats, some little prick did a slow, sarcastic clap...clap...clap.

Zaar leaned forward. "What's your name?"

"Drake..." he began, an octave higher than he intended. He cleared his throat. "Drake Callahan."

"Are you a writer, Drake Callahan?"

"Yes, sir. I mean..."

"An aspiring one, no doubt. Of horror fiction?"

"Yes," admitted Drake.

"Well, in that case, you really ought to know that the silver bullet to kill a werewolf was invented in 1941 by screenwriter Curt Siodmak for Universal Pictures' *The Wolf Man*. Siodmak borrowed it from vampire lore. Legend says a vampire must be destroyed by weapons of wood, or silver. But werewolves? The actual legends say you can kill them just like an ordinary wolf."

Drake nodded, chastened. Lesson learned. But it wasn't over.

"Tell me, Drake, do you know the two ways to become a vampire?"

"Exchange blood..." he answered, even more quietly than he intended. The assistant motioned, and he realized the mic was at his side. He raised it. "Exchange blood with one and, uh...that's the only one I know."

"Well, surprise! There's a second way. But I'll let you find that one on your own," said Zaar, now clearly enjoying himself.

Drake was homesick for his seat at the top of the aisle. Maybe if he just handed off the mic, he could return to it. But the assistant made no move—almost like she didn't want to be collateral damage—and Zaar wasn't finished. His warmly mocking tone now turned icy.

"I write horror, Mr. Callahan, but I never condescend to it. For me, it's real. That's what makes me a writer. If your idea of research ever gets past watching old flicks on television, you might actually *become* a writer."

The audience roared at that one. The shark devoured the chum.

"...and I know how humiliating it was for you," Nicole was saying.

"Do you?"

She couldn't possibly know how that long, shameful walk back to his seat had felt. It was so bad that rather than sit down, he had just kept going, out the exit. Into a torrential downpour. But he sure as hell wasn't about to go back for his forgotten umbrella.

"Okay, so I was misinformed! So silver bullets aren't in the original werewolf legends! But that's not how Zaar wrote his story. In the story, Jack needed silver. And rather than admit that he'd made a mistake, Zaar made me look like a dick."

Nicole and Odetta nodded in sympathy. Both knew Drake's anecdote by heart.

"But that was seven years ago," said Odetta. "I don't even think he remembers you."

"Why, did you tell him I'd be here tonight?"

"I mentioned your name. He didn't react one way or the other."

"See?" said Nicole. "It's no big deal."

"For him."

"You were a kid, and Peter had only hit it big a few years before," agreed Odetta. "People change. They grow up."

"He was thirty-two. I don't think a guy stops being an asshat if he's been one that long."

Odetta gave Drake a get-real look. "Honey, you did show him up. In public."

"I wasn't trying to! I just *mentioned* in passing, a mistake that he might want to fix! Oh, and asterisk? When he finally reissued the story, he did fix it. No thank-you to me in the acknowledgments, of course."

Nicole put her finger gently on his cheek, and turned him to face her. "Drake, be the bigger man. Just tell him it was all a misunderstanding, and you're sorry."

"If I'm bigger, why am I apologizing?"

"I don't know, why are you?" grinned Zaar, as he approached Drake's table, his coterie of fans following him like the tail of a comet.

Odetta turned to him with a welcoming smile. "Oh, Peter, this is Drake Callahan, a fellow author."

"I've had the pleasure," nodded Zaar. Then he noticed Nicole. He put out his hand. "But not *this* pleasure."

Nicole shook his hand.

"Nicole Finley. I'm Drake's fiancée."

Zaar took his own sweet time about letting go.

"Lucky him. And lucky *you*," Zaar added, as he picked up the lone hardbound copy of *The Monster Man*. He peered into the gap under the jacket, inspected the spine, opened and closed it a few times. Drake worked his jaw.

"Ah, the Narcissus Press," said Zaar. "I'm familiar with their work. Very impressive binding. How much are they charging you a copy?"

"I make a profit."

Behind him, Justin whispered to his pal, not nearly softly enough. "Oh, Jeez. Self-published."

Zaar handed the book back to Drake. "Glad to hear it. What was it Mark Twain said about writing for free?"

Drake met Zaar's smirk with his own set jaw. "If no one offers you pay in three years, sawing wood is what you were intended for."

Zaar put out his hand. Nicole gave Drake a pleading look. Drake dutifully shook hands, mentally steeling himself for the dagger.

"Well, Drake, good to run into you. It's been too long." He paused. "About *seven* years, right?"

There it was. Drake managed a tight smile. "They just fly by when you're not around."

Chuckling, Zaar let go of his hand.

Drake willed himself not to ball it into a fist.

Odetta put an arm around Zaar and escorted him toward the back door to the parking lot.

"Mr. Zaar has an appointment, so thank you all for coming!" she trilled to his adoring public, most of whom did not take the hint and kept shadowing him. Odetta provided blocking as best she could.

Drake glowered at the back of Zaar's head. Fortunately, for the famed author, Drake did not possess heat-vision.

From over Drake's shoulder came a callow young voice.

"Mr. Callahan? Would you mind signing this?"

Drake turned with a relieved grin, vindicated...only to see a burly Samoan deliveryman in his twenties, holding out a clipboard. On his hand truck were two large cardboard cartons with the Narcissus Press return address.

There was a laugh from Zaar's crowd. Convincing himself it was some unrelated witticism about the world of literature, Drake signed for his books.

"By the way, you owe another fourteen-fifty for the rush order."

"I paid for that on my card."

"Oh. Uh, that's not what it says here."

"Can you check with your company?"

"They're closed. Look, if you don't want delivery, I can take 'em back, and you can call tomorrow and straighten this out..."

Drake pulled out his wallet, grinding his teeth.

"I want a receipt, and I want you to write on it that I'm paying under protest."

Drake thumbed through a fat roll of restaurant and car wash coupons. He could have sworn that he'd had more than twelve dollars in this wallet. He gave up. "Can I put this on my card? Again?"

The deliveryman stopped writing the receipt.

"Sorry, just cash or check."

Nicole opened her purse and gave the man a twenty. Drake looked at the store's rear door.

Zaar, still mirthful, was disappearing into the golden haze and gray-blue shadows of late afternoon. Odetta closed and bolted the door.

Moths with their porch light extinguished, his fans flitted away in various directions.

10

MOON SHADOW

IT WAS DARK TWO HOURS LATER, AS DRAKE schlepped the two cartons to his car. Nicole opened the trunk for him and he dumped them inside. A fine drizzle was starting to stain the sidewalk. Nicole turned to Odetta.

"Good night, Mrs. Broman. So glad I could finally meet you. Drake thinks the world of you."

Odetta pulled her into a big, comfy hug. "Good night, dear. And from now on, you call me Odetta. Unless you want me to call you Mrs. Callahan."

"Thanks, Odetta."

Odetta let go, then held up a warning finger. "Now, you look after that boy. Keep him out of trouble."

"Always." Nicole climbed in the passenger side.

Drake rearranged one of the boxes. The top was open, and twenty copies were gone. None had sold, but Odetta had made him sign them. She pushed a check into his hand.

"No, no, Mrs. B, I said that you can sell them on consignment."

"That's for amateurs. You're a professional now. I'm

going to put them out on my Halloween table. And when I run low, you best bring me more right away."

He cocked an eyebrow.

"Don't you give me that look," she scolded. "I've been selling books thirty years, and some books, you just get a feeling about. Like this one. I *know* your sales are going to pick up."

"Yeah, after that rave from the dean of horror novelists."

Drake slammed his trunk shut with more force than necessary, or advisable. He turned and found himself in an enveloping hug from Odetta. Nobody since his mom had died gave hugs like Odetta.

"Don't you despair, Drake. Every true author goes through this. But can I give you a word of advice?"

He considered declining, but in that hug, he wasn't going anywhere.

"Honey, you are going to make a better writer than Peter Zaar. For one thing, you have a lot more heart. And you have an ear for how people really talk."

"Thanks, Odetta. That means so much coming from you. I want to make you proud of me."

"I am."

"I mean, *truly* proud. I want to do something...great."

"So why don't you leave the horror stuff to Zaar?"

"'Cause horror is my life!"

She held him out at arm's length, looked up at him, and chuckled softly.

"I remember. You coming into my store at nine years old, wanting to read Bram Stoker. I knew right then you were going to be a different child."

"What can I say? I like a good scare."

She leaned closer, her voice a dramatic whisper. "Then

why not write about the scary things that happen to real people?"

She sounded to Drake like she had a story in mind. He'd have to ask her about that.

"Maybe I will. 'Night, Mrs. B." Drake kissed her cheek and got in his car.

He was parked in the hollow between two vans the size of boxcars. Mirrors were useless in a situation like this, and his six-year-old car did not have a rear bumper cam. He slowly backed out onto the busy boulevard.

Odetta gasped in fright.

Drake never saw the speeding truck coming—it was decelerating from fifty miles per hour—but at the last second, with screeching tires and blaring horn, it swerved around Drake's bumper.

Everyone took a second to let their hearts slide back down into their chests.

Drake waved good-bye, and they drove off.

Odetta went back into her store to lock up. Then she went out the back way, to where her Ford Taurus was parked in the rear lot. The drizzle now made the asphalt shine.

As she pulled her key out of the back door lock, she heard something echoing on the night air. It filled her with an ancient, instinctive fear, even though she'd never heard it before, at least not in real life.

It was the howl of a wolf.

And it was near.

She debated going back inside, but the car was closer. She clicked the button on her key...but it didn't chirp. Damn! She forgot, she'd planned to replace the battery today. Still, the metal key would work.

But she fumbled it at the door and dropped the keys on

the pockmarked asphalt. With a grunt, she scooped up the keys.

And that was when she heard someone's footsteps, softly padding through the lot next door.

No, not someone. These weren't shoes. It was an animal. It sounded huge.

The only barrier between them was a wall not even as tall as she was.

Frantic, she accidentally jammed her house key into the car lock, and now it wouldn't come out! She swore and gave a powerful yank. Then one more—and this time it came out.

But now she saw a towering black shape in the lot next door. It turned in her direction, and she glimpsed a sharp triangular shape silhouetted against the rising moon. *An ear?*

The shape leapt over the wall!

Odetta jammed in the car key and twisted it—the door unlocked.

The shape charged.

She yanked the key out, tore open the door, and threw herself into the car—slammed the door behind her—locked it with her elbow.

She couldn't see the shape clearly now—her windshield was blurred by the falling mist. But she knew she had time to do only one thing: She could either grab her cell phone and dial 9-1-1, or she could handle this herself.

The shape came closer to the misted glass. As it did, its moon-shadow came into focus. She saw it clearly now, a lupine silhouette, taller than a man.

She jerked open her glove compartment, grabbed the snub-nosed .38, and swung it toward the dash.

The windshield exploded in a shower of safety glass, and she shrieked.

11

WITH HIS OWN BLOOD

"The Church's one foundation,
Is Jesus Christ, her Lord.
She is his new creation,
By water and the Word.
From heav'n he came and sought her,
To be His holy Bride,
With His own blood He bought her,
And for her life He died."

MARIA'S VOICE WAS FULL, AND SHE DID THE soaring Wesley melody proud. She ended with a mighty sting from the pipe organ that shook the dust off the rafters of the old wooden church.

The young priest was tall and barrel-chested, with freckles and a curly thatch of copper-red hair.

"Ah, that was wonderful, Maria. The angels are jealous. Why don't you take lunch now? You must be starving."

"Thank you, Father Kevin!"

The fortyish Latina crossed herself and walked to the

back of the church, leaving the priest sitting in the front pew with Nicole and Drake.

"It's a lovely hymn," nodded Nicole. "And she played it beautifully."

But Drake could tell her heart wasn't in it. He took the bull by the horns. "Kev, I wonder if..."

The priest indicated the departing organist, and murmured softly. "I'd prefer you call me Father Kevin in public, Drake."

Drake chuckled, good-natured.

"Dude, what the f...?" Recalling his surroundings, Drake quickly shifted gears: "...*hell?* We've been friends all our lives."

Kevin's expression discouraged further chuckling. "Inside the church, we're not friends."

"But this isn't my church. I'm not in your congregation."

"No, but you did ask me to officiate at your wedding."

"*Nicole* asked you."

"And you agreed. Call it professional courtesy, if you like. But you need to show me the proper respect."

"Buddy, I respect the bejeezus out of you, but I'm not..."

Drake stopped.

Nicole was silently imploring him.

"All right, fine. Father."

"Thank you," said Father Kevin. "Now, I realize a lot of your guests are not Catholic, so I'm trying to be broad-minded about the music."

Drake was diplomatic. "I did notice that. I mean, that's actually an Anglican hymn. So I appreciate the spirit of diversity and outreach. But I don't think that a song with the words 'blood' and 'died' in the first verse is appropriate for our opening number."

Nicole silently cringed.

Kevin's patience was thinning like lake ice in April.

"This isn't Vegas, Drake. Our weddings don't have an opening number."

"Poor phrasing. My bad. But Nicole really wanted something, you know, romantic. She had her heart set on 'Can You Feel the Love Tonight?'"

"That's a show tune. From a Disney cartoon."

"Hey, *my* nominee was 'Put a Ring on It.' If I can give up Beyoncé, you can compromise, Kev."

"*Father Kevin.*"

"Goddamn it, I can't call you 'Father.' I've known you since kindergarten. And I'm six months older than you."

Kevin started to rise to display the full effect of his height and weight advantage. "And yet, I was always able to kick your—"

Nicole cleared her throat.

Kevin also recalled his surroundings, and his collar. He sat back down, trying to channel his inner Bing Crosby. "Well, that was a long time ago. We've both changed."

Nicole leaned between them, blocking their mutual stares. "You said you had to counsel us before the wedding. That's what we're here for. This is not about converting Drake. And Drake, I'd really appreciate it if you would not take the Lord's name when you're right in front of the altar."

"Sorry, sweetie."

Father Kevin kept his eyes on Drake. "Nicole, could we have a minute? I want to counsel Drake one-on-one."

Drake didn't look overjoyed, but he nodded at her, as if to say, it's okay.

Kevin gestured at the entrance. "I left the *Times* out in the narthex, if you want to read something."

"Is this going to take *that* long?" she asked.

Kevin gave Drake an appraising look. "I don't think it *has* to."

Nicole knew her brother well enough not argue. She nodded dutifully."Thank you, Father." She rose and slid out of the pew past Drake, adding, "You boys play nice."

Nicole crossed herself and walked up the aisle. On her way out, she picked up the newspaper. At the door she paused, then went back for a short pencil from the visitors card basket, and headed outside. She had a feeling she'd have time to do the crossword.

As soon as she was out the door, Kevin lasered in on Drake. "Tell me again why you want to marry my sister."

"You know damn well why. Because I love her. I have since I was old enough to know what love is."

"I remember the summer she came back from camp, and she had blossomed. I knew right away you were infatuated with her." Drake started to protest, but Kevin held up his hand. "I know you feel a deep, respectful friendship for her and genuine affection. And of course you're physically attracted to her. But I have to ask, do you genuinely love everything about her?"

"Is this leading to anything besides one of us getting a punch in the nose?"

"Calm down. I just want my sister *and* my best friend, both to be happy. I want her to find her soulmate. I'm just not convinced that's you."

"Lucky for me, you don't have to be. We can go to Vegas and get married."

"You really think that's the way to make her happy?"

Drake looked down and expelled a breath. "No. She really wants your blessing. She wants your dad there. She wants a big family wedding in your church. And I'd like *my* best friend and brother-in-law to be there for us. So why are you holding this over our heads?"

"Because I know my sister. Nicole is deeply spiritual. Her faith is central to her."

"I respect her beliefs, and she respects mine. Come on, you're one of the most liberal guys I know and *the* most liberal priest. You fight for the poor, you protest every war, even the popular ones. You got in hot water with your own church for turning in that pedophile priest...are you actually telling me you won't officiate at an interfaith wedding?"

"If you were a devout Jew, or Muslim, or Mormon, or Buddhist, at least I'd have some hope. Some common ground. But you have *no* faith."

"For the same reason I don't have a tail—I don't need it. I rely on knowledge. On experience. On science and physics and reproducible experiments. On logic and mathematics. Things I can see and feel or figure out on a piece of paper."

"Plenty of scientists are Christians," said Kevin.

"*Are* they, by your definition? Look, I always admired Jesus. That's never changed. It's why I follow his moral teachings. Why doesn't *that* make me a Christian? Why do I also need to believe in magic? That he walked on water, or cursed a fig tree, or rose from the dead, or resurrected Lazarus? Or that Moses parted the Red Sea, or that God created the Universe in six days?"

"If you were even agnostic about it...if you had an open mind, I could work with that. But you've shut me out on this since we were thirteen."

Drake, Kevin, and Nicole had grown up attending this very church. But in Drake's thirteenth year, he'd formed fatal doubts, and when the time came for him and Kevin to take confirmation, Drake refused.

And then he stopped going to church.

The irony was that something had happened to both of them that summer. Drake had lost his faith. And Kevin had found his.

Kevin had never been much for the Bible as a boy, but that June, on the second anniversary of his mother's death, he went for a rare bike ride alone, without Drake. Kevin churned up the park road so fast he thought his heart would burst out of his chest. When he crested the hill at the top near the Observatory, there was truck careening toward him on the wrong side of the road. It didn't honk or brake— Kevin swerved and jammed his pedal down for speed, but he knew he was dead.

And yet, the truck missed him. By a hair.

That was when Kevin had his epiphany. He braked at the side of the road. Half stepped, half fell off his bike, and walked to the edge of the cliff overlooking the whole L.A. basin, and the vast ocean beyond.

And Kevin knew the presence of God.

No booming basso voice, no choir, no angels or burning bushes. Simply a palpable glory that lit up his mind with a sense of the eternal.

Maybe, Kevin thought, it was like the vision quest that he'd read about American Indians having, one that was different for every person.

All Kevin knew, from that day on, was that he had found his calling. He would be a priest. He had been given a great gift and it was up to him to share it as best he could.

When he tried to explain it to Drake, it was like trying to describe color to a man born blind.

His best friend responded to Kevin's revelation by suggesting it was "a psychotic break." The little wiseass was always coming up with jargon like that. When Drake said that God was a superstition dreamed up to comfort scared cavemen, it had hit Kevin hard.

Even harder than he hit Drake, if that was possible.

It was the worst fight they ever had. Kevin felt sure if he didn't do something, Drake was going to Hell. Kevin loved Drake like a brother and when you're thirteen, it's still possible to believe you can physically knock some sense into your brother.

Even then Kevin had a big size advantage, but Drake managed to sock him in the nose hard enough that Kevin had to let him up.

They didn't speak for months afterward.

The worst summer of their lives dragged by, interminable.

One day, Drake went out riding his bike, starting from Ferndell and going up into the hills of Griffith Park. He'd ridden it countless times, with Kevin always in the lead. It was a hellishly hot, lonely ride by himself.

When he got to the parking lot at the Observatory, there was Kevin, on his bike, taking in the clear view of Catalina Island afforded on a blustery Santa Ana day. They'd come up in opposite directions, and arrived a minute apart. Drake didn't know it, but it was the very spot where Kevin had had his epiphany months earlier.

They were both too exhausted to ride any further, so they both stayed.

Drake still couldn't remember who had spoken first.

Maybe it was only a grunt that led to a one-word observation, then two words...

And then before they realized it, they were talking. About the heat, the view, the Planetarium show, the heat, the meteor shower that night, an upcoming bicycle race, the damn heat again, how great it would be to ride way the hell down Olympic, all the way to Santa Monica Beach and jump in the ocean. Everything but their fight.

Finally Drake said, "Kev, let's just never talk about church or God or any of that crap again. I don't want to lose my best friend over that."

Kevin nodded. "Okay. Let's go to the beach."

———

And for the next thirteen years, they had stuck to that bargain. Until now.

"Drake, just tell me one thing. What makes you so unwilling to admit that there might be a God?"

"Because you, and the Church, and everyone else says that God is omniscient, omnipotent, and all-loving...but that just can't be. Birth defects, babies dying, goddamned plane crashes! Cancer, earthquakes and tornadoes, floods and fires, war, torture, genocide! A God who knows about all this suffering, and has the power to prevent it...and doesn't...that is not a loving God."

"You're trying to judge God. To understand the infinite with a finite mind. You're talking about terrible things. But I could tell you stories I've seen with my own eyes. People doctors gave up on, cured by prayer..."

"Or the power of their own belief."

"If you want to call it that. But there's more: The way God works through people to do things they never thought they could. Inspiring them to create great works of art, giving them the strength to endure or to sacrifice for others, or to forgive and be healed, or comforted in tragedy. A million everyday miracles..."

"Christ, Kevin, you know goddamn well why I'm an atheist! The wonder of it is that you *aren't!* Your mom...my Cub Scout den mother, our school's room mother year after year, head of the church auxiliary, volunteer for every charity in town, for God's sake...as sweet and kind a woman anybody ever knew...went on Nicole's Brownie picnic and got struck by lightning! How the hell am I supposed to put my faith in a God who does shit like that?"

Drake stopped, choked up.

Kevin misted up too, but kept his voice calm. "How? By recognizing that you're *not* God. And that we cannot understand His ways."

"You and I are different people, buddy. If I can't understand something, I can't have faith in it."

"What are you going to tell your children when you have them? That either their father or their mother is wrong?"

"I'll take them to church. Just like I went. You and Nicole can tell them what you believe. But I'll also tell them what I know about life. One way or the other, they'll figure it out. They'll find their way."

Kevin looked at him and said nothing.

Drake returned his gaze, determined. Then he added: "There is one thing in this world that I do have absolute faith in: I love Nicole. And if I'm lucky enough that she wants to marry me, then maybe...*maybe* there is a God. Don't you think that's enough?"

Kevin regarded him for a long beat, then sighed. "I'm going to consider you a work in progress. I'll expect to see both of you here in church on Sundays."

"Sundays," repeated Drake. As in every Sunday? Well, he thought, marriage is about commitment. "All right. We'll be here."

They rose and shook hands. Drake's cell went off, loudly. Kevin fumed.

Drake smiled, embarrassed. "And this'll be off."

Drake saw the caller ID. "What's up, Lisa?"

When she told him the news, he cried.

12

ANOTHER WOLFBANE MOMENT

P ARKING AT BROMAN'S BOOKS WAS complicated this time by half a dozen black-and-whites, plus the coroner's car and the transport van, which were now blocking the alley that led to the rear parking lot.

Drake couldn't bring himself to look into the cadaver pouch for more than a few seconds, just long enough to identify the remains of Odetta Broman. Then the investigator mercifully zipped it up.

Drake wiped his eyes with his sleeve. "Jesus Christ, I can't believe it. I just talked to Mrs. B last night."

Lisa nodded. "Seems like you're the last one who did. Did she say anything about someone she might be meeting?"

"No, she was just going to go home. Said her feet were killing her. Of course, they always were. Oh, God."

Lisa felt she needed to be something besides coolly professional. She put an arm around Drake's shoulder in an awkward side-hug.

"Chen, who is this man?"

Lisa dropped her arm.

Drake looked up at the owner of the sharp voice. It belonged, appropriately, to a sharp-featured, fortyish face—long, lean and bony, with skeptical eyes that seemed to call you a liar before you opened your mouth.

"Um, Lieutenant Ed James...Drake Callahan, our consultant on lycanthropes. He noticed the wolfbane in the flowerbed."

"Oh, I see." Lieutenant James sounded halfway impressed. He shook hands. James was wearing a disposable latex glove. Drake rather hoped James hadn't touched anything infectious yet.

"He was also a friend of the victim."

"He a friend of yours, too?" asked James.

"Yes, sir."

"Should I have someone else interview him?"

"No, sir. Anyway, his fiancée was with him and can confirm his story."

"I'll want to talk to her."

"Yes, sir."

Suspicions apparently allayed, Lieutenant James put a territorial foot on the low brick planter behind the building, and turned his full attention to Drake. "Well, Mr. Callahan, if our killer runs true to form, we have one more night before he vanishes for a month. What can you suggest?"

Drake cleared his throat but couldn't get the thickness out of his voice. "From what I've read, these killings have all occurred within a five-mile radius and in or near the hills."

"Well, with one exception, up in Tujunga."

"Tonight, if I were you, I'd pour a lot of cops into Hollywood, Silver Lake, Echo Park, Los Feliz, Atwater Village..."

"We've been doing just that. Officer Reyes was killed up on Beachwood Canyon before he could fire a shot, as you might recall from yesterday. Any other ideas?"

"Maybe, keep them in pairs?"

Lieutenant James' stare suggested that he could see something repulsive inside the back of Drake's skull. He gave Lisa a mirthless grin. "Good to know the department's money has been so well spent." James walked off.

Lisa knew she would hear more about this later.

Drake shook his head, amazed. "Your boss is quite a dick, isn't he?"

Lisa shrugged. She couldn't exactly agree with so many other cops within earshot. "Drake, it's just, he has to okay your fee. I really could've used another wolfbane moment."

"Sorry, Lisa. I..." He swallowed. "That's one of my oldest friends in that body bag. I'm whatever I am today because of her. I'm not exactly focused on botany right now."

Not that there was much in the way of vegetation in the little parking lot. Just a scrawny box hedge that was starting to yellow. To Drake's disgust, he realized there were red drops on some of its oval leaves.

But then he looked closer. Inside the top of the shrub was wedged a business card. He recognized the cream shade and the distinctive Bookman font. Drake fished it out of the branches.

As he'd figured, it was Odetta Broman's business card. He couldn't repress a shudder at seeing a tiny drop of blood on it. He turned it over, and in handwriting (not hers) was jotted an address: *2495 Glendower Drive*.

"Hey, Lisa, look at this."

Out of nowhere, Lieutenant James' latex-covered hand abruptly plucked the card from his fingers. "We have rules about how to handle evidence, Mr. Callahan."

"Who knew it was evidence? Your guys must've missed it. But you're welcome for the address."

Lisa opened a manila envelope. James read the back of

the card, then dropped it in. "Catalog it anyway, but it's a dead-end," he told her.

"What does that mean?" asked Drake.

"It means we'll handle this from here, thanks," said James, looking off.

"Like you guys handled the Laurence Maher case?"

Another story Drake had followed in the news: The latest celebrity wife-killer case had just gone to the jury after some compromised physical evidence and a parade of prosecution witnesses who could have climbed out of a clown car.

At the mention of the Maher case, James glared at Drake: if looks could maim, Drake would have needed a wheelchair.

"Get him out of here," seethed James.

Lisa escorted Drake from the parking lot to the alley.

"Good going," she said between closed teeth. "James was on the Maher case."

"Huh. Why doesn't that surprise me?"

"I really wish you hadn't said that to him. All the bad press is a really eating at him."

"If he doesn't get off his ass, he'll be reading about how he blew *this* case too."

"Drake!" She rolled her eyes, exasperated. "Do you ever get tired of talking yourself into trouble?"

"You know what 'in trouble' is? When some billionaire bible-thumper slices up his wife, and the DNA evidence just *happens* to decompose at the police lab."

"You are way out of line!"

"Relax, Leese. I'm not a reporter. I don't give a rat's ass about the department, or James, or the preacher's wife. I just want to find out who ripped my friend open like that. Do *you* recognize that address?"

"No, I don't."

"Well, aren't you curious why James blew it off?"

"The lieutenant is the lead detective on this case. If he says it's nothing, trust me, it's nothing."

"This isn't about trusting you. You're asking me to trust *him*. No thanks."

Lisa held her temper. "Drake, go home."

Drake walked back to his car, fuming. As he did, he pulled out his pen and notebook and wrote down "2495."

13

LYCANTHROPY

THE CRACKED CONCRETE STREET HUGGED THE hillside as it wound past expensive old Mediterranean homes. The houses themselves were on small lots, and dated back before World War Two, but now they all had multi-million-dollar views of Los Angeles and, on a clear day, the Pacific.

An Internet search had revealed little except that the four-bedroom, six-bath house at 2495 Glendower had last sold a dozen years earlier to Argent Associates, a corporate non-profit, and was not available for rental.

The two-story structure faced south. It was painted a traditional weathered ochre. It was set back twelve feet from the road, with an abbreviated front yard behind a low wall. Driving slowly past the house, Drake could see that behind the home lay more grass and a compact, oval pool with a new cover. Beyond that, the backyard abruptly rose to become a steep, ivy-covered slope, with bare dirt and exposed rock at the top of the hill.

Drake had parked fifty yards away, far enough that he was not conspicuous, but still had an unobstructed eyeline on the entrance to the house. He watched all afternoon, as the sun set.

The house was well-maintained, and looked lived-in: its tropical plants recently watered, its window shades open. But it lay silent, no movement visible within. No one had come in or gone out during his surveillance.

At one point, Drake had left his car and knocked on some nearby doors, passing himself off as a realtor, but only two residents had answered, and both disclaimed all knowledge of their neighbor's identity.

Once it was dark, Drake walked onto the property. No interior or exterior lights came on.

Drake had begged off meeting with Nicole and their wedding photographer to do his little stakeout. By this hour, she would be having dinner with her father, which Drake was also supposed to have attended. Jack Finley was undoubtedly using the occasion to advise his only daughter not to marry an unreliable writer.

Well, Jack kind of had a point, thought Drake. His reconnaissance mission had blown a lot of good will and come up empty. He wondered what the hell else he could accomplish here.

Drake had never broken and entered before, but inspired by movies about burglars, he was dressed all in black, including a leather jacket he'd seldom had occasion to wear but seemed somehow right for this. He zipped the jacket halfway up against the nighttime chill.

He told himself he wasn't actually committing burglary, since he had no intention of setting foot inside the house and tripping an alarm system. But he could easily get close enough to sneak through the yard, peer in the windows, and perhaps find some kind of...something.

There was no streetlight nearby, and the moon had yet

to rise. Drake was halfway up the short driveway when headlights raked the upper story. A car was coming—and as it rose around the curve of the road, Drake saw the light-bar on top.

Cops!

Drake dove over the wall and flattened himself in the dichondra. He listened to tires slowly rolling by. After a minute, the car sounds receded and the beating of his heart drowned them out. He peeked over the top of the wall and saw the cop car vanishing around the bend with two officers inside. At least James had listened to him on that score.

Once the cruiser was gone, Drake turned to the dark house. Keeping low, he knelt by the front window and shone a bright halogen beam into the living room.

The furnishings told him nothing, except that the decorator had had a generous budget and a taste for antiques. Nary a magazine lay on the coffee table. Then Drake saw a bookshelf adjacent to the window. He could just make out the titles.

The owner had to be a horror fan: Expensive hardbound editions of the founding giants: Mary Shelley, John Polidori, Edgar Allan Poe, Bram Stoker, Robert Louis Stevenson, H. G. Wells, Lord Dunsany. And somewhat faded, shabbier volumes...could these be first editions? The names on the spines were Arthur Machen, Algernon Blackwood, H. P. Lovecraft, August Derleth, Ray Bradbury, Robert Bloch.

And of course, well-represented were the modern masters: Stephen King, Clive Barker, Dean Koontz...and depressingly, every damn book Peter Zaar had ever written.

A gust of cold wind blew up from the ocean, but it was something else that chilled Drake's spine in this moment: the unmistakable sound of a door creaking open.

He whirled his beam to the front door.

It was now ajar, moving slightly in and out with the wind. No one was there.

Drake cautiously moved onto the tiled walk leading to the door. He aimed his flashlight into the inky void beyond. A light suddenly shone back at him!

He jumped back, and the light moved in tandem with his own.

A goddamn mirror.

He must be crazy. It was time to turn around and leave. But what was he afraid of? Arrest? Damn right! He was already trespassing just being in the yard! But then he remembered his last look at Mrs. B, in the cadaver pouch. He wasn't going to wuss out now, not with an invitation like this. He put one foot inside.

He froze at hearing a buzz.

From his cell phone. Again, Drake waited for his heart to slow. He saw the call was from Nicole. She'd have to wait now. He shut down his phone so it couldn't ring again.

Then Drake entered. He swept the hall with his beam. There was a hall table, but no mail on it.

Aside from the occasional sighing of the wind, and the door swaying in response on its poorly lubricated hinges, the house was soundless as a tomb.

Drake's heart was throbbing, but he kept telling himself there was no danger. If the Full Moon Killer truly lived in this house, he certainly wouldn't commit murder here. So for the next few hours at least, this house was arguably the safest spot in Los Angeles.

Using his jacket sleeve to avoid leaving fingerprints, Drake pulled the front door shut with a soft click. He should have brought gloves, but since he didn't even own a lock pick set, he hadn't foreseen his getting inside the house.

He passed the living room. Next on his right was a

dining room, also opulent, dark and seemingly unused. A tiled 1930s kitchen lay beyond that.

Lighting the cracks around the door at the end of the hallway was a faint bluish glow.

Drake slowly pushed open the door, which mercifully was better oiled than the creaking front door. Beyond lay what appeared to be an artist's studio with a northern exposure.

The room was pitch black, except for a bank of tall windows and French doors which looked onto the narrow backyard, whence came the illumination: The full moon had just climbed above the eastern hills, rim-lighting the tops of trees, and painting everything outdoors in cobalt shadows.

He wanted to flick on a room light, but with cops patrolling the street, and with neighbors home, that seemed unwise.

His halogen beam picked out another bookcase—this one with horizontal glass doors on each tier. In it were crammed musty volumes, some of them dating back a century or more, and more than a few in languages Drake did not even recognize.

One glass door was open and shoved back, and a medical volume lay fallen on its side. In new black ink, the spine read: LYCANTHROPY. Drake owned the same book.

The realization that he must be in the home of a completely self-aware, self-diagnosed serial killer made Drake shiver.

He saw weapons of bygone ages mounted on the wall: a mace, a broadsword, a crossbow loaded with a wooden bolt. These did not appear to be stage props but genuine antiques with the rust and dust of centuries on them.

A muffled growl outside startled him. He flicked off the flashlight, held his breath, and listened intently.

He hadn't heard a dog earlier. Not even at the neighbors' homes. For half a minute, he waited. But he heard nothing more, besides the wind.

Drake took a step forward and knocked his knee painfully against something heavy. He flicked on the flashlight again and found it was a large tank of oxygen. Seeing a tall lamp, he decided to risk better illumination, and turned it on.

The oxygen was paired with an acetylene tank, sitting beside an oak desk covered with a thick sheet of glass. Atop that sat a jewelry torch hooked up by hoses to the tanks, a porcelain crucible, and inside that, a crucifix, half-melted into a puddle of now-solidified silver.

Drake carefully felt the end of the crucifix. He applied some force. It bent easily. Pure silver, it had to be.

There was also an open can of black powder, empty brass cartridges, and a device Drake had never seen, though he had a guess as to its function. He grasped the mechanism's wooden handles and opened it. Out plopped a tiny, gleaming silver projectile with a rim around its base.

This was a bullet mold.

And next to it...

A revolver.

There was nothing else on the desk, except for a lone piece of printer paper with ten shaky, hand-printed words:

PLEASE DO IT FOR ME
I DONT HAVE THE GUTS

Drake picked up the revolver. Could it really contain silver bullets? He wanted to check, but wasn't sure how to open the thing. Finally, he noticed a rod on the frame just forward of the cylinder. He slid it out, until the cylinder fell open, revealing a full load of shiny-tipped bullets. Too shiny to be lead. Drake held them up to the lamp for a closer look—

—just as a wolf howl erupted right outside the house.

Jolted, Drake lost his grip and dropped the pistol. It glanced off the desk as it fell, and all six cartridges clattered onto the floor.

That same moment, Drake glimpsed something taller than a man in the backyard, standing erect. The moonlight tipped its fur with silver, but the rest of it was a murky blue-gray. Its ears were pointed, lupine, and even in this darkness, its eyes were lit up a demonic red.

Drake dove for the cartridges. He scooped up three or four and, with frantic fingers, began to shove them back in the chambers. He had only two reloaded when the dark figure leapt through the French doors, shattering them into a thousand flying shards.

A snarling seven-foot werewolf crashed down in the center of the room and strode right toward Drake.

He snapped the cylinder closed, pushed in the rod, and aimed the gun—the monster knocked it aside with ferocious power—BANG! The shot went wild, blasting a hole in the paneling as the gun flew from Drake's fingers.

The thing with a wolf's head opened its maw to rip out Drake's throat. Drake grabbed the desk lamp and held it out. The beast closed its jaws, biting the lamp in two—it shorted out in a shower of sparks and a pungent sizzle of flesh as the room went dark.

The beast roared in pain and gave a vicious swing of its

—hand? forepaw? Whatever it was, it knocked Drake across the room.

Drake landed headfirst against the glass-fronted bookcase with such force that the shelves collapsed in a pile of books, splintered wood and broken glass.

Dazed, Drake crawled from the wreckage. His head was aching from the impact. He could feel his ear had been cut, and his shoulder, right through the leather jacket. Then he remembered—the gun! Where the hell had it landed?

The next instant, sharp claws whipped him onto his back and the slavering muzzle of the beast appeared inches above his face, emitting a guttural growl, a snarl peeling its mouth back to expose dagger-sharp white fangs. Drake groped around with both hands in a blind panic, searching for the pistol. Broken glass sliced his finger.

Miraculously, amid the books and the debris, his left hand felt the barrel, and he closed his fist around it.

Before Drake could do another thing, the beast's claws seized his jacket and dragged him to his feet.

The werewolf opened red jaws to rip Drake open. But in that final second, Drake got the gun turned around and fired point blank at the monster's heart.

The beast gave a shrieking howl, mortally wounded. Then it went limp, releasing its grip on him as it slumped to the floor.

After what seemed an eternity, Drake realized he was still standing in pitch blackness. He stumbled over the ruins of the bookshelf to the entryway and groped around the door jamb for a wall switch.

Somewhere in the distance, a police siren wailed, grew louder...and closer.

Drake finally found a switch. He flicked the overhead

fixture on. He wanted a good look at this thing, even though he knew damn well what it was.

It wasn't human, but it wasn't a wolf either. It was some horrible amalgam of the two that walked erect. Well, up until a few seconds ago.

He was still trying to wrap his mind around the fact that he had nearly been killed by a creature that three minutes ago he was absolutely certain was a myth, and that now lay dead on the...

What the hell?! If this was a dead werewolf, it wasn't going to look like one for long!

Drake patted himself down, anxiously seeking his cell phone. He found it but—damn it! He'd turned it off! Now he turned it on and waited agonizing seconds for it to reboot.

But during that time, the shape on the floor was already shifting. The fur shrank into the skin, the hind legs and paws were losing their lupine bone structure and reforming into human legs and feet. The fangs were rapidly sinking back into a snout that was itself dwindling into what would soon be a human face.

No, no, no! Hurry up, you obsolete stupid-phone! He needed proof!

The siren cut out as the cops skidded to a halt outside.

Now the phone gave its "all ready" chirp and he shifted it to camera mode.

But by then, the transformation was complete. The last fur and fangs had receded and all that was left was a bloody, nude male form with a hole in its chest and the familiar, devilishly handsome features of...

Peter Zaar.

Drake winced. "Oh, *shit*."

14

BUSTED

"WE HAVE WITNESSES WHO SAW YOU two quarrel at the book store!" insisted Lieutenant James, his voice pitched at just the right volume to make the knot on Drake's head throb.

"We did not 'quarrel'!" said Drake, his own volume adding to his discomfort.

"Then why did you go to his house?"

"I didn't know it was his house. It was the address on Mrs. Broman's card. As you damn well know!"

Tom Callahan gave his brother a kick under the table.

Lieutenant James could not suppress a flicker of a smile. He kept pushing. "Tell us again, what happened after you broke into his house."

Drake opened his mouth but Tom's voice beat his by a second.

"Don't answer that. He didn't break in, Lieutenant. He already told you, the door was open."

"The first officers on the scene said it was locked."

"He pulled it shut out of concern that someone else might enter who was *not* a good Samaritan."

"Good Samaritan? Is that what you call shooting a man in his own home?"

Despite all of Tom's warnings, Drake was losing his temper. "I had no reason to kill Peter Zaar, and you know it."

"Our witness said he made you look like a fool. And that the bookstore owner took his side."

"Like hell she did."

"And she wound up murdered, too. You know, I think we need to have another talk with that girl of yours and see if she still supports your alibi for last night. Or, maybe, wants to tell us the truth."

Drake leapt up from his seat. "You want the truth? You want to know what really happened?"

Tom gripped his arm. "Drake, shut up, and sit down!"

After a long moment, Drake obeyed.

Tom turned to Lieutenant James and Lisa. "I need a minute with my client."

"You *had* a minute," said James. "You had twenty."

"And you've had two hours with him. If we're going on a long fishing expedition, I hope you brought beer and sandwiches. Or are you planning to charge him?"

There was a long pause as Tom and James glared across the table at each other. Then Lisa broke the awkward silence.

"I think we can give them a bit longer, sir."

Drake saw James shoot Lisa a look. But she was playing good cop, of course. And as thoroughly as James was playing bad cop, the game required her to show she could back the bad cop off, at least temporarily.

Finally, James nodded, and rose. "You have five minutes. Not six, not five-and-a-half." He yanked open the door to the hallway.

"And would you mind turning on the lights in the room behind the mirror?" added Tom, mildly.

The vein at James' temple pulsed, but he said nothing. He turned on his heel and walked out.

Lisa relaxed a bit. "Of course, we'll do that. But you ought to know we would never violate your privilege."

"Of course," said Tom.

Lisa left the room. A second later as promised, the observation room on the other side of the one-way glass lit up, to reveal Lisa with her hand on the switch, then withdrawing and shutting the door.

Only now did Tom turn back to his brother.

Drake let loose his anger. "God damn it, Tom, I saw what I saw."

"Guess what I saw, on my first day in criminal law class? First day! Professor Hallman is taking roll, and suddenly a guy in a hoodie runs in. He pulls out a .357 Magnum and swings it around the room. A woman in back of me screamed.

"The guy yelled, 'None of you muthafuggas move!' He grabbed Hallman's briefcase and ran out. It was over in about six seconds.

"Hallman then asked us to write down a description of the suspect. We all did. And just about every one of us blew it. I didn't even get his race right. Most of us didn't. I thought he was black, about six-two. When he came back in with the briefcase, it was a white guy, maybe five-nine. And that .357 Magnum? It was actually a snub-nose .38."

"Tom, what does that—?"

"That taught me a great lesson about how unreliable eyewitnesses are. How traumatic events can erase memories, or make them fill in details that never existed."

Tom hovered his finger near Drake's bandage. "Especially after a serious blow to the head."

"I didn't imagine the silver bullets, did I? Why would Peter Zaar be making silver bullets?"

"Oh, who knows? Maybe your idol Zaar went psycho writing all that supernatural crap—a word to the wise, little bro. Maybe he *wanted* someone like you to kill him. Maybe this was all some sick plan. Suicide by rival. I don't know, and neither do you, except that all that crazy stuff he had there helps us—it supports the idea that Zaar was not rational."

Tom got up and leaned over Drake in his chair. "You were assaulted and injured tonight, by a man who would have killed you if you hadn't killed him first. And you're still in shock. So...let's stick with the events that we know, logically, realistically, must have happened." Tom ticked them off on his fingers.

"You found a card with an address. You were suspicious. You showed up at Zaar's house without knowing he lived there. You saw the open door and entered out of concern something was wrong. He threatened you..."

"Stop writing my testimony for me!"

"Then he attacked you. You feared for your life. And you got to the gun first. It was self-defense. Isn't that the only real way it could have happened?"

"You're close. Except, we didn't say a word to each other, and I didn't know he was Zaar...because he was a goddamn werewolf!"

Tom blew out a breath, and sat back down at the table to regard Drake. Drake had only been twenty when they lost their parents in that plane crash. Tom was four years older. But dragged out of his house at midnight to bail Drake out of this mess, Tom felt the gap between them was more like fourteen years. Or forty.

"Use your head, Drake. The best thing to tell them is, your head hurts, and you just can't remember much right now."

"Tom, you're telling me to lie!"

"Why did you call me tonight, Drake?"

"Because you're my brother. You're all the family I have left!"

"No. You had one phone call, to get a lawyer. That's what I am right now. I've been giving you my best legal advice. Yes, I'm your brother. And I'd walk through fire for you, but the only way Mary and I will be at your wedding next week, is if you listen to me *as your attorney*. If you tell the lieutenant out there the same hallucination you told me two hours ago about a werewolf, there is not going to be any wedding. Because you will be in a rubber room at County."

Drake searched his brother's face for sympathy. "Tom, I swear on my life, it's true. It happened. Don't you believe me?"

Tom ruffled Drake's hair, lovingly. "Dude. Of course I don't. But I'll get you the best shrink in town."

The door opened and Lieutenant James returned, alone. He sat down and opened his file folder.

"Let's go over your whereabouts, starting with July 30th."

"Don't answer that," said Tom.

"Why not?" Drake asked his brother.

"Because you'll be helping them lay out a timeline that could frame you, goddamn it!"

Drake turned to James. "I have nothing to hide. I was at the Hollywood Bowl with Nicole and about ten thousand witnesses."

Then Drake stopped, as his recall kicked in. "Wait. You

said July? That was when the Full Moon murders began, right?"

"You tell me."

"'Cause Peter Zaar got back from his European book tour on July 29th."

James looked up, intrigued. "Did he? Sounds like you were stalking Peter Zaar. Is that what you've been doing?"

"Don't be a dumbass," snapped Drake.

Tom massaged his brow. He was coming down with Drake's headache.

James went a little purple. "What did you call me?"

Tom rose. "I think we're done here."

"The hell we are," snarled James.

"You think you have enough to charge my client?" scoffed Tom.

"You bet your ass" said James, glaring at Drake. In a comic strip, you'd depict it with a line of tiny daggers.

At this juncture, Lisa entered with a printout. She cleared her throat. "Sir, you should see this. The coroner's investigator found some blood in the master bath shower."

James turned his little daggers on Lisa.

She forged ahead. "It's a very rare type, AB-negative. Not Zaar's blood-type. Or Mr. Callahan's. But it was Odetta Broman's. The lab's running the DNA now to see if it's a match."

Tom simulated innocent surprise. "Ohhh! Like, maybe *last* night, the dear, departed Mr. Zaar had to wash some blood off him that came from a murdered woman? Huh. That's wild. Know what I think, Lieutenant?"

James, stony, did not venture to mind-read.

"I think, instead of grilling my client as a suspect, you'd better get ready to pin a medal on him for stopping a serial killer."

Lieutenant James closed his folder and muttered to Lisa. "Kick him loose."

Tom rose, amiable. "Well, that's almost as good. But I hope there will be a medal ceremony at some point, Lieutenant. Let's go, Drake."

Tom clapped Drake on the shoulder. Drake got up. Lisa held the door open, but before she could follow them out, James addressed her.

"Detective, I'm wondering if I need to reassign you to a case where you don't have a conflict of interest."

"Sir, I don't have one here."

"I hope not, for your sake. Lieutenant Gutierrez recommended you be put on desk duty until this Jarrett investigation is settled. I'm beginning to think he's right."

"Sir, my total focus is the Full Moon Killer."

James regarded Lisa stonily, then gave her an admiring nod. "I heard what you did to that human stain. If it was up to me, *you'd* get a medal."

Lisa wanted to smile, but it didn't feel professional. "Thank you, sir."

"Get back to work. You came highly recommended for your work on cybercrimes. I need to know what's on Zaar's computer. Report back directly to me."

15

BY THE BOOK

THE OCEAN VIEW FROM GLENDOWER STREET was awesome, but Lisa didn't have time to appreciate it. She rubbed her eyes, then resumed scrolling through the files on Zaar's top-of-the-line laptop. It was nice. It had a wireless link to the huge high-res screen on his desk, and in general, made hers look like a Flintstones computer with rock handles.

A voice behind her made her jump: "Hey. Thanks for getting me sprung."

Lisa turned `to see the last person she wanted to see just then. She looked around, hoping none of the cops or forensic investigators knew who Drake was.

"You should *not* be here!"

Drake smiled at her concern. "I'm fine. I just had to see the place in daylight. I need to make sense of what I saw."

"That's not what I meant! How the hell did you get in?"

Drake showed her Tom's ID badge from the Hollywood station.

"They forgot to take it when he left. I borrowed it off his coat when he drove me to my car."

"You *are* aware that taking things that aren't yours is against the law?"

"I'm returning it!"

"Yeah, right. By the way, in case it wasn't obvious...James fired you. Now give me that. You are still a person of interest." Lisa took the ID badge.

"What do you mean, person of interest? I thought Zaar was your killer."

"Looks like. But there's a lot of weird stuff we can't explain yet."

An investigator walked by with a man's hand in a plastic evidence bag. Drake barely managed to avoid vomiting. He took a deep breath.

"Weirder than loose human body parts?"

"Yeah. Like, what happened to all Zaar's money? Every bank account I can find is just about tapped." Lisa opened another tab and scrolled through data.

Drake frowned. "He had fifteen bestsellers. They make movies of anything he ever wrote. Thank-you notes, grocery lists. How could he not be loaded?"

"That's what I wondered. He didn't even own this house. It's paid off, but it's owned by one of his trusts, to be maintained after his death as a museum, in perpetuity. And as for the rest...?" She turned her palms up.

"Maybe it all went for silver bullets."

Lisa snorted. "Not even. That bullet you drilled Zaar with? We dug it out of the wall. It was good old-fashioned lead. Like the rest of them are—lead, with a little silver paint. See?"

Lisa opened an envelope and dumped several bullet out onto the desk.

Drake leaned in close, and saw where the shiny paint

had been scratched off...showing dull gray lead beneath. "What the hell?"

Lisa could tell he was worried. "What?" she asked.

"Well, if I didn't shoot Peter Zaar with a silver bullet... then maybe he's not dead."

Lisa gave him a sidelong look. "Oh, he's dead all right. Please tell me you are not worried that he really was a werewolf."

Tom's warning haunted Drake. "What would you say if I said I *was* worried?"

Lisa took Drake by his shoulders, heart-attack serious. "I would say, don't let Tom talk you into some kind of insanity defense. Even if it worked, you'd wind up in a booby hatch instead of walking free. So play it straight and don't be a schmuck."

"Yeah. You never were a believer in the supernatural, were you, Leese?"

"Uh, *no!* And neither are you, as everyone knows. That's why you better not try and pull that crap."

"Yeah, I figured. Okay." He paused. "But you're absolutely sure he's dead."

"He better be, the coroner sliced open his chest. I'm told it was a pretty incomplete job. We had orders to fast-track the autopsy."

"Why?"

"I'm not sure. What I heard was, it's in Zaar's will, he has to be buried by sundown today, for religious reasons."

"Except, Zaar wasn't Jewish! He wasn't any religion. He was a lifelong atheist!"

"What are you, his biographer?" asked Lisa.

"Lisa, when is the funeral taking place?"

"What do you want to know for?"

"I just want to pay my respects."

"You didn't exactly respect him. You called him an insecure, overrated hack."

"Come on, you owe me a favor. I need this," said Drake.

"And I need you out of here, before you get me suspended."

"Hey, who gunned down your serial killer for you?"

Lisa put a finger to her lips. She continued, voice low. "It's all pretty hush-hush. As soon as the coroner confirmed the bullet passed through Zaar's heart, he got orders to sew him back up. Right after that, the funeral home picked up the corpse. Don't ask me who ordered that. It was not what you'd call by-the-book."

"Lisa, this is important! I have to find out where he's being buried. And when."

"Drake..." she began, irritated. But she could see desperation in his eyes. "Okay, I'll try."

"You have to promise me. I need it before dark!"

"If I promise, will you get out of here, right now?"

"It's a deal."

"I'll call you later. But don't tell a soul. Got it?"

"Absolutely. On my landline, though. My damn voicemails keep getting lost."

Drake turned to leave, but he noticed something on one of the bookshelves. All the other volumes had a fine coat of dust, except one leather-bound tome.

There was no name on its spine. Drake pulled it out, and found the title on the front cover. The letters were embossed in gold leaf:

Вулкодлак

"Lisa, look. Someone was reading this pretty recently. My money would be on Zaar."

"What does it say?"

"The letters are Cyrillic. I kind of know the alphabet. Their B is our V. The one that looks like Pi is L... And that one's D. So you'd pronounce this: 'vil-kod-lak.'"

"Meaning?"

"*Vlkodlak* is a Slavic term for werewolf."

Lisa gave him a warning look.

"Hey, he's the one with the crazy books," shrugged Drake.

"Can you read it?"

Drake flipped through the pages. "No, I'm not even sure what language this is. But my money's on Bulgarian."

"Why?"

"Because one of the scheduled stops on Peter Zaar's book tour was the city of Varna in Bulgaria." He paused. "And after Varna, he came home early."

"Now I *know* you were stalking Zaar."

The voice was not Lisa's. Neither was the hand that snatched the book from Drake's grip.

Both belonged to Lieutenant James. He thrust the book back into its place on the bookshelf.

"Chen, what the hell is this man doing here?"

Lisa kept her cool. "Just turning in this ID, sir. His brother accidentally walked out of headquarters with it."

James pocketed the ID badge and fixed Drake with a baleful stare.

"Get this straight, Callahan. You are no longer consulting for this department. You have no business at any crime scene. Do I make myself clear?"

"Crystal," said Drake.

"Good," said James, turning to a uniformed officer who looked fresh from the academy. "Get him out of here."

James headed upstairs. The officer took Drake by the arm.

"Gee, thanks, Tenderfoot, but I don't need your help crossing the street," said Drake.

Lisa gave Drake a warning look. The cop tightened his grip.

Drake tensed. "Are you going to let go, or do I call my attorney?"

Drake yanked his arm free with great vigor, just as the policeman let go. Drake wound up stumbling against the bookcase, knocking several volumes over. Fuming, Drake picked them up and shoved them back upright.

"You touch me again, and you're going to have one sweet lawsuit," he warned.

Unimpressed, the officer reached for his arm again.

"All right, all right!" said Drake, backing away.

The policeman gestured at the door.

Drake straightened his jacket and marched out with as much dignity as he could muster...considering he had a cop shadowing him, one pace behind.

It was three minutes after Drake and his escort left that Lisa noticed the empty, clean slot on the otherwise dusty bookshelf.

16

VLKODLAK

COURIER TYPEFACE, BLACK ON GLOWING WHITE, announced the website, "On the Same Page: A Writers' BBS." The reference to a page, the old typewriter font, and indeed, the idea of a computer bulletin board service, were all nostalgic avatars of earlier times. Yet it was very modern in effect: Even in car-crazy L.A., Drake knew most of his fellow authors only electronically.

The hundred or so working novelists, screenwriters, playwrights and journalists who regularly logged onto OTSP were a brain trust he could turn to whenever Google failed.

Alas, his new thread, "Anyone Know Anyone Who Can Translate Bulgarian?" had already been read by thirty-eight members, and so far, the only comments were from wiseass comedy writers ("Yes, but only into Albanian," "Gzbyftk!" and "You should have learned her language before you sent her the plane ticket.")

"Ha, ha," muttered Drake.

It would be hours before he got a usable reply. He grabbed the remote and clicked on the news.

He was comforted to see Sydney Jackson, his favorite local newswoman, doing a stand-up in front of Superior Court downtown. Like any working TV journalist, Sydney was ridiculously attractive, but like an actual reporter, she asked incisive questions, and she clearly had legal training. She was African-American and had an endearing habit of turning her final d's into t's, like pronouncing her own name "Sytney."

"The jury has ended its second day of deliberations in the trial of televangelist Laurence Maher. It was one year ago this week that his wife and co-star Lola Maher was stabbed to death outside the couple's Hollywood Hills mansion."

The newscast cut to B-roll from Maher's show, *Doing the Lord's Work.* There was Maher, smug, pink and plump, with helmet-hair and a silk suit no doubt priced at a couple grand; he still looked like a hundred dollars. He was fighting back glycerin tears as he addressed the camera:

"The Lord told me if my flock doesn't tithe as He has commanded that He will have no choice but to call me home."

Maher's fleshy wife Lola leaked mascara in rivulets as she wailed to the heavens about God's fatwa on her husband.

"Please, Lord, give us another chance! We need our shepherd's guidance! And, folks, we need your donations!"

It was an appalling spectacle, and Drake had nothing but contempt for the way these two had sheared their flock over the decades. But poor Lola hadn't deserved to have her throat slashed open, and there was no doubt in Drake's mind that it was her dear hubby Laurence Maher who had sent her butchered to her Maker.

The film then cut to footage of Lola's funeral, with Laurence looking just as convincing as bereaved husband as he had as God's intended sacrifice.

Sydney narrated over the footage. "*At first, a drop of Lola Maher's blood that police said was found on her husband's shirt was seen as ironclad evidence. But alleged contamination of the DNA evidence at the LAPD lab has hurt the prosecution's case.*"

A key turned in the door of the guesthouse, and the door swung open. Nicole entered carrying their boxed wedding cake.

Drake leapt to her aid. "The cake! Oh, goddamn me, I totally forgot."

"It's fine, honey. You've had a terrible couple of days. No need to swear."

"Let me move this and you can set it down."

Drake worked his left hand under a pile of papers on his dinette table, clapped his right on top, and transported the entire mess, intact, to his desk chair.

"Thanks," she said. "I ran out of room in my fridge, with all the champagne and the food for the reception. Tom said we could use his deep freeze, but they're out tonight."

Nicole set the cake down. Drake was already removing shelves from his mini fridge to make room.

"I'll get it over to him first thing tomorrow. I'm sorry about the photographer. And dinner with your dad. I promise, starting tomorrow, I'll be back helping you full-time."

He removed the shelves and slid the cake into the fridge, which was four feet high. It just barely fit...after he plucked the bride and groom figures from the top of the cake. Conquering the temptation to lick the frosting off their feet, he laid them in the freezer compartment.

Nicole sank into a dinette chair, exhausted. "Drake, I'm worried our wedding is going to be a disaster. Maybe we should just postpone it until we can afford a wedding coordinator."

"No!"

"Daddy said he'd pay for the whole thing if we just waited another six mon..."

"No! No way! We don't want his bribes. We can do this! We've done most of the work already. And you've done an *amazing* job. Those blue bridesmaid dresses you made are awesome!"

"Aw, thanks, darling." She sank her chin into her hands and closed her eyes. "Ohhh...right now I could sleep on a clothesline."

"Why don't you lie down and have a nap?"

"I can't. I'm just going to rest my eyes a sec."

Drake turned back to the TV, where Sydney was still dissecting the Maher case.

Eyes still closed, Nicole murmured. "Oh, yeah, the florist called...he can't get blue flowers."

"Oh, for God's *sake!*"

Nicole opened her eyes. It was gratifying that Drake was taking the wedding arrangements so seriously, but really? The flowers were what bothered him?

Then she realized he was yelling at Sydney Jackson, wrapping up her report on TV.

"*...and there have been no requests to review exhibits or testimony, further fueling court watchers' opinions that this will be a hung jury.*"

"It's open and shut, you gohmerts!" groaned Drake. "Guilty! What is it with L.A.? O.J., Baretta, now Laurence Maher...if you're even a bit famous, knock off your wife in Tinseltown and you walk!" Drake clicked off the TV, fulminating.

Nicole sat up, and put a gentle hand on his shoulder. "I can see this touched a nerve."

"It's just that celebrities are like 007—they have a license to kill. But let a nobody like me dare to shoot a famous guy

—who's trying to kill me by the way—and it's 'Throw away the key!'"

"You're not a nobody."

"Tell that to my agent. She quit today. Told me she can't do any more for me. I'm radioactive. Looks like I killed my book deal along with Zaar."

"But that is so unfair! It was self-defense! Didn't Tom say you don't need to worry?"

"Yeah, so he says."

She kissed him. "Then just take it easy, honey. There'll be other agents and other deals. The important thing is, I know you're innocent."

Drake wanted that to be enough. It wasn't, however. "But you think I hallucinated that werewolf."

"Well, yeah...what else *can* I think?"

"Oh, I dunno. I guess you're right. Tom says the same thing. I just wish I could make myself believe that."

That reminded Drake—he needed to put the tripod and camera in the car. He slipped his Flip video cam into his pocket, and grabbed his tripod.

"I'm going out to my car for a sec." No point telling her all about his little mission, until it was accomplished. She'd only worry.

"Oh, Drake, I picked up your tux—it's in my car. But I didn't lock it."

"Thanks! I'll get it."

He kissed her, then headed out the door. Nicole watched him go. Then she noticed something rolled up in newspaper in the sink.

She unwrapped it to find a big bouquet of blue wildflowers. The weight lifted from her spirits. What an incredibly thoughtful guy she was marrying! How could he possibly have known about the florist? Or, was this just Drake's little gift, because he knows how much she loves blue? Well, best to let him spring his surprise. She carefully rolled the blooms back up into the business section.

The land line rang. Nicole tried to pick her way around the cartons of books, but the machine picked up before she could get there. Drake's outgoing message was brief.

"It's Drake. You know the drill."

Then came the message. Nicole recognized Lisa, speaking in a low voice, as if she did not wish to be overheard.

"It's me. Mountain View Cemetery, tonight at six. Our little secret, okay?" Click. The message light started to flash.

Nicole went cold all over.

She went outside.

She walked down the long driveway, along the board fence that separated the rest of the backyard from an old kidney-shaped pool filled with slightly chartreuse water. Out beyond the front house, on the street where she'd parked her car, she found Drake bent inside the open door, removing his tux.

He shut the door and turned—and jumped at seeing Nicole inches from his face.

"Whoa! Nicole, you oughta be a ninja! I didn't even hear you."

She searched his eyes. "Drake, tell the truth. Have I been driving you crazy?"

Drake slipped his arms around her waist and pulled her close. "Hell, yeah. Ever since you were sixteen."

"I'm serious. If you have any doubts about our getting married, I want..."

"What? No!" Slow and emphatic, as if she were fresh off the boat: "We. Are. Getting. Married."

Nicole nodded, seemingly reassured.

Drake kissed her gently. "Is there anything else you want brought in?"

Nicole shook her head. "You go ahead. I'll get it."

"'Kay." Drake carried his tux into the guesthouse.

Nicole watched him go and chewed her lip.

When was he going to show her the flowers?

Coming in the door, Drake saw the blinking light on his venerable Panasonic. He pushed playback.

"It's me. Mountain View Cemetery, tonight at six. Our little secret, okay?"

Drake checked his watch. It was almost six now, but he didn't need to be there for the burial service. It was what might happen at moonrise that concerned him. Plus he had to make a stop first. He heard Nicole's approaching steps. He sure didn't want to explain to her what he was about to do. He erased the message just before Nicole entered.

Drake grabbed his coat from the brass hook. "I have to run out and see someone. About some research. You're welcome to stay."

Nicole shook her head.

"Okay, you've got your key to lock up?" he asked.

She nodded.

He grabbed the rolled-up newspapers from the sink and pecked her on the cheek as he rushed out.

He didn't even notice the look on her face.

Father Kevin stared at the altar. On the left side stood the heavy antique Spanish candlestick. Thirty inches long, taller than was really practical, a bit wobbly, but it was beautiful. It was one of a pair donated by a parishioner whose family went back in Los Angeles to the Spanish land-grant days. The candlestick did too. Alas, its mate, which had been there this afternoon, was now gone.

"I came in to practice," stammered Maria. "I saw right away that it was missing. Oh, Father Kevin, I'm just sick! Who would do such a thing? Steal from a church?"

She crossed herself.

"Well, it's very *Les Miz*. I can only pray that whoever took it had as much need as Jean Valjean." Father Kevin paused, working his jaw. "But if he comes back for the other one, he's going to need a trip to Lourdes."

"That is strange, isn't it?" said Maria. "Why did they only take one candlestick?"

"Maybe that's all he needed. Or maybe he just was in a rush." The priest sighed. Humanity kept finding new ways to disappoint him. "He sure knew what to take," he said. "The most expensive things on that altar. Solid silver."

17

PERMISSION

A LOVELY OLD HAND-WROUGHT SILVER candlestick, nearly as long as a baseball bat, sat on freshly-laid sod in the little graveyard.

Tucked away between big film labs and warehouses in an industrial zone of Hollywood, just blocks from Kevin's church, Mountain View Cemetery was the best-kept secret in Movieville. No famous stars were buried here to inspire pilgrimages; no summer movie screenings were held on its weedy grass. It was owned by the Diocese and had served the parish for over a century before it filled up and became just a costly drag on church finances.

Then a decade ago, the on-site crematorium had run afoul of California environmental laws; with the land still zoned for cemetery use, its removal had opened up another half acre of plots. Parishioners got first dibs; non-parishioners were welcome, but required to pay a hefty premium. Not much of a bargain, considering there was only one full-time caretaker, Seamus, who was now seventy, and who usually passed out in his little cottage by the gate before seven P.M.

The fence, which these days was more ivy than chain link, was easily scaled, as Drake and Kevin had proven many times as boys; Drake felt sure some ghoulish fan would soon steal the new polished marble plaque set into the grass:

PETER ZAAR — Author

Why the hell would a big shot atheist pay through the nose to be buried in this rundown little churchyard?

The guy probably *was* broke, if his other business decisions had been as sound as this one.

It hadn't really been a funeral. Just a simple interment of a polished mahogany coffin with what looked like gold handles and fittings—the bastard did have style, thought Drake—and not a single mourner in attendance. Unless you counted Drake, watching through the fence. Seamus had filled in the hole, laid down the turf, left the hose trickling and called it a night.

Seamus had also neglected to padlock the gate, saving Drake the trouble of climbing the fence.

Drake placed his blue flowers around the mound so they touched each other. Then he screwed the tiny Flip cam onto the tripod and aimed it at the grave. He picked up the silver candlestick, and feeling only mildly idiotic, pressed the record button, turned on the timer code, and stepped into camera range.

"Friday, seven P.M. The first night since I shot Peter Zaar, the first night since his rushed autopsy and funeral. I dunno why I'm doing this. It's two nights since the full moon. Maybe the moon isn't full enough to bring back a werewolf. Or maybe there's no such thing as a werewolf, and Peter Zaar is dead, and the whack on the skull he gave me is the only reason I thought I saw one. If so, I'll delete this file, and we'll fill up the memory card with our wedding video." He started out of frame, then stepped back in.

"But on the off-chance that Peter Zaar does not rest in peace...I want proof."

He checked his watch. "The moon will rise in—"

SNAP. A twig broke right behind him.

Drake whirled with the candlestick, ready to bash in the brains of—

"Nicole!" He stopped the candlestick an inch from her head, then dropped it in shock.

"Goddamn it, what are you doing here?" he yelled, his heart fibrillating.

But then he saw the tears in her eyes.

"Are you cheating on me?"

"Am I what?"

"With Lisa?"

"*What?* No! She's a pal, like Kevin! Jesus, Nicole, you *know* I've known her since kindergarten."

"Drake, I heard the message she left."

Oh, damn, realized Drake. I thought it came while we were both outside. This is what I get for being the last guy in America with an answering machine.

"She tells you to come here, you bring flowers...*blue* flowers! Like we wanted for the wedding?" Nicole's pitch rose, vulnerable. "You have another explanation, right?"

Drake paused. "Ye-eah. But you're not going to like it any better."

Then Nicole's gaze fell to the ground and saw the blue blossoms patterned in a precise oval.

Now she was spooked. "Drake...why did you arrange our flowers around this grave?"

"These are not for our wedding. They're wolfbane. It's a

circle of wolfbane, to trap Zaar. If he's really a werewolf, he won't be able to cross it. I think."

"You mean, if he rises from the *grave?*"

"Yeah. When you say it...I have to admit, it sounds a little crazy. Especially when you're looking at me like that."

"Oh, my God, Drake," she said, shaking her head. "You need help."

"I'm not insane! I just need to know for sure. One way or the other, I swear this will be over tonight. Do you trust me?"

"More than anyone I know."

"Then please go home," he said.

"Let me wait with you."

"No!"

"Why not?"

"Because," Drake began reluctantly, "what if what I saw wasn't because of a blow to the head? If there's even one chance in a trillion that what I saw was not a hallucination, I want you safe. I want you miles from here. Will you please, please, this one last time...*just humor me?*"

He sounded scared. And that scared her.

"All right. I'll go home. If you promise to come by and see me, as soon as you leave here. Okay?"

"I promise."

She walked away, then came back, took off her crucifix, and put it around his neck. "Humor me. 'Cause I want *you* to be safe." Then she kissed Drake tenderly and walked out the gate.

Drake watched her taillights dwindle into the night. Then he sat down on a headstone and waited. A light breeze kicked up.

The moon would not rise for another hour. Drake checked his phone, but there were no bars. In the heart of industrial Hollywood? That did it; screw his plan, he was signing up with CREDO first thing in the morning.

Half an hour was a long time to sit on someone's tombstone in the dark with nothing to do. He wished he'd brought a book. Well, he was a writer. Maybe he could write a story about a guy waiting in a graveyard? Yeah, that had never been done before.

The old pepper trees shook their tiny dry leaves longer with each new wind gust. The news said there would be a lot of wind and rain after midnight. He hoped the guesthouse wouldn't lose power. He zipped up his jacket.

Then he noticed the mist.

It wasn't foggy anywhere else in the cemetery. Only here, right above the...

Oh. My. God.

The hair on the back of his neck rose.

White mist was swirling up from the fresh-turned earth on Zaar's grave.

Only the mist didn't blow away. It just gathered, condensed, darkened...until it formed the shape of a man.

To be specific, Peter Zaar in his black funeral suit and black overcoat. He had a ghastly pallor, and his fingernails were long and pointed like blades.

He saw Drake...and smiled. Showing his fangs.

Instead of screaming, running, or fainting, Drake's remarkably calm first move was to think: I'm pretty sure wolfbane works on vampires too.

And indeed, it would have. Except that the wind had blown a flower away from his barrier of monkshood.

And over that break in the circle, Zaar stepped off his grave. He clucked his tongue at Drake's carelessness.

Drake brandished the silver candlestick. "Get the hell away from me!" He swung the candlestick.

Zaar jerked back an instant before Drake would have brained him. The vampire curled his lip. "Don't flatter yourself, newbie. You're not my type. But, that hot fiancée of yours..."

Whoosh! Drake swung at Zaar again. Zaar again ducked, but this time Drake connected with the Flip cam. It was a home run. Drake lost it in the dark.

And when he looked back, Zaar was no longer in front of him.

Instead, Zaar was on the other side of the gate, where Drake's car was parked.

Drake ran as fast as he could, but before he could get there, Zaar rammed a sharp finger into the front tire— BANG! It went flat. Then BANG! He did the same to the rear tire.

Drake got to his car, winded. It was undriveable. Zaar was gone. But a huge bat was flapping up into the sky, making a beeline for Beachwood Canyon.

Drake speed-dialed Nicole. He got three fast beeps.

NO SIGNAL. CALL FAILED.

He jumped in his car, gunned the engine, and roared away up the side road towards a main street, the car sagging to one side, screeching as he drove on his rims. He kept hitting the call button, but the call kept failing.

Drake emerged from a canyon of warehouses and turned right onto Santa Monica Boulevard. A customer pumping gas at the station on the corner looked on in panic as Drake squealed his car to a halt, spewing sparks.

Smoke from his wheels filled the station. Drake jumped out and walked away to where he could breathe. This time he could hear a ring on his cell. He waited, muttering, "Nicole, for God's sake, pick up!"

Instead, he got her voice mail:

"It's Nicole. Leave a message, text me, or write me a nice letter!" (Beep!)

"Nicole, I know it sounds nuts, but Zaar is not in his grave! He's a vampire and he's coming after you! But the legend says he can't get in if you don't invite him. Call me back!"

The customer at the pumps was now gaping at Drake, who was still yelling into his cell: "Whatever he says, *don't ask him in!*"

A gleaming red Maserati GranCabrio swept up to the next island. A thirtyish man in a suit that cost more than Drake's car got out. Drake was immediately in his face.

"Mister, please, I need a ride to Beachwood Canyon. It's an emergency! My girlfriend's life is in danger!"

The young man, who had to be an agent, gestured at his car. "Does this look like a taxi?"

"It's close enough," said Drake, swinging him out of the way and shoving him into the window-washing stand. The squeegee handle snapped off, black water sloshed all over the agent, and blue paper towels fluttered everywhere as Drake leapt into the car and tore off toward Vine Street.

As the owner's colorful curses faded into the distance, Drake tried Nicole again, but got voice mail again. He clicked off, then speed-dialed Lisa.

"What's up, Drake?"

"Can you get to Nicole's apartment, like now?"

"I'm about five minutes away. Hey, it sounds like you're driving. You have any idea what a cell phone ticket costs?"

"Shut up, this is important!"

"Drake, do I hear sirens?"

She did. Drake already had two LAPD cruisers on his tail. He didn't care.

"Shut the hell up and listen! You have to get to Nicole's apartment before he does!"

"*Who?*" demanded Lisa.

"A guy who's trying to kill her, okay?! This is important: tell her to put on another cross."

"Did you say a cross?"

"She gave me hers!"

"Drake, what the hell—?"

"Just tell her!"

Drake dropped his cell to focus on swerving through an intersection where the light was red. The car handled like a dream, though he lost the passenger-side mirror to a parked truck.

Nicole came out of the bathroom in her sleep shirt and a terry robe, with a towel around her wet hair.

She saw the missed call from Drake on her phone, but before she could pick it up, she heard a tap at her sliding glass door.

Puzzled, Nicole looked out onto her patio. Fog swirled. She couldn't see anyone. Tap! Small white pebbles, the kind that lay on the building roof, were hitting the glass. She rolled the heavy door open two inches—as far as it would go without lifting the "burglar-proof" wooden dowel out of the tracks.

"Who's out there?"

"Nicole. Let me in," said a voice out in the mist.

"Who is that?"

"You know my voice. I'm Peter Zaar."

Nicole exhaled in irritation. "Right. Good impression, Drake. But you don't scare me."

"Good. Open the door, and tell me I can come in."

"Come in, Drake. But only ten minutes. You're not staying."

"No."

"What do you mean, 'no'?"

"You have to say, 'Come in, Peter Zaar.'"

"This is not funny! I was worried about you. Sitting in that creepy graveyard!" Her tone softened. "Nothing happened, right? You're okay? Didn't see any more werewolves?"

"I can honestly say I didn't. But we need to talk about what happened. Please. You have to say it, or I can't come in."

Nicole began brushing her hair with a vengeance.

"You and your dumb stories!" she muttered under her breath.

"Please, Nicole. It's a matter of life and death."

Nicole smacked down the brush on her night table, aggravated.

"Oh, for the love of…all right, fine!" She bent over, removed the dowel, slid back the door, and rolled her eyes.

"Come in, Peter Zaar."

Mist blew in off the patio, surrounding her. It wasn't that cold a night, but the mist made her shiver uncontrollably—it was freezing.

Lisa dashed up to the building. She tried Nicole on the intercom. Getting no answer, she dialed the on-site manager, who reluctantly buzzed the door open.

Just then, Drake screeched to a halt and abandoned the

Maserati in the middle of the street. Lisa tried to ask him what was wrong, but he rushed past her and dashed down the hallway. The two units pursuing Drake skidded to the curb, sirens cutting out but radio chatter filling the street.

"Unit 104!" she shouted to the cops as they ran to the door. She dashed down the hall ahead of them.

Drake's key worked but the chain deadbolt was on. Drake kicked Nicole's door. The jamb cracked but the woodscrews held. Drake kicked it again, splintering the jamb—the door flew open. But at that second, two brawny cops caught up to him and grabbed his arms. Drake thrashed violently, but he couldn't get loose. Lisa stepped in the doorway and froze.

Then Drake saw what she saw.

An animal wail of grief tore from his throat.

Nicole's naked body, a deathly white, lay flat on the living room floor, facing the patio door—her ankle was wrapped in the taut electrical cord of her phone charger. Her head had crashed through the glass door just above floor level, and lay impaled on the broken glass of the frame. Her throat was gashed open, and what little blood was left in her was dripping outside, into a drain on the patio.

There was no question that she was dead.

"Nicole! Oh, God, no!" sobbed Drake, fighting to get free. The two cops slid and cursed, barely able to hold him.

"Keep him back!" ordered Lisa. "Nobody goes in until I say!"

There was something odd about this crime scene. If that's what it was.

Lisa looked out on the patio, but all she saw was thick white fog, blowing off the deck and into the night.

18

—————

NO WEDDING AND TWO FUNERALS

THE FINLEYS WERE WELL REPRESENTED AT THE funeral and for the burial in the family plot at Mountain View. But Drake's only blood relative in attendance was Tom, there with his wife Mary. Lisa stood with them.

"I take it Drake's not coming?" Father Kevin whispered to Tom Callahan.

Tom shook his head.

Kevin shrugged. "Well, maybe that's for the best. Dad doesn't want him here. I begged him to postpone this a few days, but you know my dad."

"I don't think a few days would make any difference," Tom replied. "Drake won't answer his phone. He hasn't set foot out of that guest cottage. Won't even open the door. Says he's doing 'research.' I'm worried about him."

Lisa glanced around at the old tombstones. "Did you know he was here when Nicole died? He had some crazy idea that Peter Zaar was going to come back from the grave. He even called Nicole to warn her."

Tom winced. "No, I hadn't heard that. This is all my fault.

I thought Drake would get therapy on his own. I should've had him committed."

"That wouldn't have helped," Lisa said. "Drake had absolutely nothing to do with her death."

"I wish you could convince Dad of that," said Kevin. He looked over at his father, Jack: Red-faced from weeping, but the whiskey he'd been drinking all day was not helping. Kevin's uncles were propping him up.

When Kevin's mother died, Jack had been a tower of strength for his two children. But now, burying his daughter beside his beloved Kathleen, Jack was a wreck.

"I told your dad," said Lisa. "I was the first one on the scene. The door was locked from the inside. The patio door was blocked. And Nicole had vacuumed before she took her shower. The carpet pile was up, and there wasn't a footprint anywhere, besides hers. No one else was in there, unless he was on wires."

"So, Nicole just tripped over a power cord?" marveled Tom's wife. "That's so weird."

"It was just a freak accident, Mary. There's no way it could've been anything else."

"If you're so sure it wasn't a homicide, then why were you pushing Dad to do an autopsy?" asked Kevin.

"Because it might have turned up...I don't know. Something. Some condition that might have contributed to her fall. Anyway, he wouldn't hear of it. And your dad's word carries a lot of weight in this town."

"That it does. Well, I can't wait any longer. I need to start the service."

After Kevin's eulogy, their cousin Bridget sang Leonard Cohen's "Hallelujah." There wasn't a dry eye in the cemetery.

Until Drake walked in the gate. He wasn't crying. He looked numb. And grimly determined. He wore the same jeans and button-shirt he'd been wearing the night Nicole died. He hadn't shaved, and smelled of sweat and coffee and taurine. He clutched several sheets of printed text in his hand.

Jack and various other Finleys kept shooting poisonous glances at Drake.

Bridget continued her song.

Tom gave his brother a sympathetic nod. Mary hugged him, but he barely seemed to feel it. Stone-faced, Drake stood beside them.

Lisa eyed him with concern, then leaned in close to whisper. "Are you okay?"

He shook his head.

"What is it?" she asked.

"Zaar said there was a second way, but I didn't find it out till too late."

"Second way to do what?"

"Turn vampire."

Tom glanced over at Drake, his heart sinking.

Drake ignored him. "That volume from Zaar's library. I finally got it translated. *Vlkodlak* means both werewolf and vampire. In Slavic folklore, they're two stages of the same creature. Like caterpillar and moth. When the werewolf dies, it becomes a vampire. That's what Zaar meant by there being a second way."

He drew a ragged breath.

Lisa looked at him pityingly.

"And that's what Zaar is now. And Nicole is dead

because I didn't protect her. Because I didn't know the damn legend."

Tom took firm hold of Drake's shoulder and spoke under his breath. "Bro, listen to me closely. I had to do hand-springs to keep you out of jail. You're now about to land yourself in the psych ward."

Drake shook off Tom's hand. He walked over to the dirt pile where Seamus stood waiting, grabbed the shovel out of the old gravedigger's hand, and walked off.

"Drake?" said Tom, a warning tone in his voice. "Where are you going?"

"I'm going to cut off his head and ram this through his goddamned heart." Drake broke into a run.

Tom, Mary, and Lisa raced after him.

Kevin gave the fastest benediction ever.

"ThepeaceofGodwhichpassethallunderstandingkeepy-ourheartsandmindsthroughChristJesus, amen."

Kevin crossed himself then dashed after them, vest-ments flying.

Seamus hobbled along, bringing up the rear.

Drake rounded the corner of a crypt and came to a halt beside Peter Zaar's plaque, now lying in the roadway. He gaped at the grave, stunned.

The newly-laid turf had been torn asunder and peeled back, as if from an eruption. The straight walls of the freshly-excavated grave were visible five feet down into the churned-up dirt.

Drake jumped into the hole and shoveled the loose earth madly. But there was nothing else in the grave. No coffin. He dropped the shovel and sank to his knees, sobbing, exhausted.

Tom reached down his hand. "Come on, Drake. I'll take you home." He pulled Drake out of the hole, and he and Mary walked his brother toward the cemetery gate.

"Was there an order to exhume Zaar?" asked Kevin, *sotto voce*. Not so sotto that Drake didn't hear it.

"No," said Lisa.

Drake turned back to hear more, but Tom gently tugged him along. "C'mon, bro. You're coming home with us."

"Leave me alone, Tom!"

Tom tried to hug Drake, but he shoved Tom's hands off him and marched out the gate to his car.

Tom started to follow, but Mary held him back. "Honey, he's not going to listen to you. Give him some space."

Seamus ambled up the path to Zaar's gravesite and retrieved his shovel. He took his time, eavesdropping as Kevin and Lisa stared into Zaar's violated grave.

"There was no exhumation order," continued Lisa. "I would have heard about it. But on the other hand, this looks too professional to have been dug by some vandal or grave robber."

The gravedigger cleared his throat.

Kevin gestured at him. "Oh...Lisa, this is Seamus Riley, our caretaker."

Seamus doffed his cap, and spoke with a lilting brogue.

"Caretaker, stonemason, gravedigger, gardener, professional mourner, bartender for wakes...you name it, I do it."

"Did you have something you want to tell us, Seamus?" said Kevin.

"If ye'll pardon me, Father, from the looks of it, this grave wasn't 'dug up' at all."

Kevin and Lisa exchanged a puzzled look.

Seamus took his shovel, and made a deep vertical cut down to the base of the dirt pile, then dragged away the compacted chunk of soil, creating a cross-section that ran all the way down to the grass. At the base of the dirt was the new sod, lying upside-down, mashed into the grass below by the weight of the soil.

"D'ye see how all this dirt is packed together like this, like it's all one layer? We had us some rain late last night, and it soaked about two foot into the soil."

"Yeah, I see. "

"Well, this is upside-down now. The wet soil is on the bottom, and the dry soil is on top. Ye can see the line where it stops right there."

Kevin saw. Plain as day. "What does it mean?"

"Well, if someone'd shoveled this dirt out, or used my backhoe, it wouldn't be flipped over neat like this. The wet soil, and the dry, would have gotten mixed together, 'cause it'd take several goes, even with the backhoe."

Lisa was getting impatient. "So if this dirt wasn't dug up, how did it get here?"

Seamus raised his palms over his head, his stubby fingers touching, then spread them apart.

"It's more like this was...*pushed* up from below."

19

A KNOCK ON THE DOOR

Drake looked up at the ceiling. He couldn't remember how long he'd been lying on his bed, staring at the ceiling. What day was it? Sunlight streamed through venetian blinds. It was definitely full daylight, and someone was pounding on his door. But who? Drake couldn't think straight. He wearily rose and approached the door.

"Drake, come on, it's me!" It was Nicole's voice.

Oh, my God, was today the wedding? Had he overslept? He wasn't even dressed!

Drake yanked open the door to find Nicole in her wedding gown. It was like some Art Moderne throwback, white and streamlined so it flowed over her, dazzling in the sun like radiant liquid silk.

And her face...she looked like an angel.

Drake looked in the mirror by the door, and realized he had nothing to worry about—he was already wearing his wedding tux, with the white bow tie.

"Nicole!" he breathed. "They say it's bad luck to see the

bride before the wedding, but I don't believe it for a second."
He was so relieved, he started to cry. My God, the nightmare
he'd just had...about her death.

"Come on, everyone's waiting for us!" she urged.

Drake was speechless with joy. If only somebody would
stop that damn pounding.

Drake's eyes flew open.

He was lying face up on his bed, as before, but it was
pitch black outside.

In a horrible rush of awareness, Drake realized he'd only
been dreaming. And what in his dream was only a vague
nightmare of Nicole's murder—that was his reality. And
would be for the rest of his life.

So he lay there, weeping.

And the goddamned pounding on the door went on.

"I'm coming, I'm coming, damn it!" He wiped his eyes on
his shirtsleeve, and went to the door. He whipped it open
to see...

Nicole.

Standing in the dark, in that same silky wedding dress
she'd been buried in. A bit dirty around the edges. She
smiled, revealing elongated canine teeth.

Oh, call them what they were:

Fangs.

"Aren't you going to ask me in?"

Drake had left a cup on the hall tree. It still had water in
it. He dashed it in his own face, sputtered, looked again.

She was still there.

"*Nicole?*" She nodded, but made a face. "That name has

always made me sound so...proper. Why don't you just call me Nikki?"

Drake couldn't take his eyes off her. She was Nicole...and yet, not. Even when she wasn't showing her fangs, there was the alabaster-pale skin, contrasting with wild, lustrous black hair and those deep red lips. Her lashes were longer and darker too. Her eyelids looked like she was wearing blue eye shadow, but he could tell she wasn't. Her formerly brown irises had a reddish hue, while the whites of her eyes seemed to glow. She was definitely more a Nikki than a Nicole.

Her dress clung to lush, mushrooming curves in a way he'd never noticed before. She wasn't merely beautiful. She wasn't just alluring. She was hypnotic. Irresistible.

"O-kay, Nikki. You know you're a vampire, right?"

She smiled, wryly. "Yeah, I figured, when I had to fog my way out of my coffin."

"Oh, God. A vampire can't enter any place without permission. Why did you let him in?"

"Well, he *said* he was Peter Zaar, but I thought it was just you messing with me. Doing voices. Like you *always* do."

"What? But that isn't fair!" sputtered Drake. "You didn't believe him. That's not genuine permission to enter. That's not informed consent!"

"Yeah, but he's not a lawyer, honey. He's a vampire. Who are apparently more unscrupulous. Anyway, look at me. It obviously worked."

"And he made it look like an accident, so no one would autopsy you. I guess he made you drink *his* blood?"

"Yeah."

"That life-sucking scumbag *bastard!* That blood-gorged human tick! Goddamn his untalented ass to hell!"

Nikki poked him in the ribs, right where he was ticklish.

"Look at you, all jealous! It's not like I went all the way with him. It was just a little harmless blood-drinking. It didn't mean a thing. I don't even like him. Why are you so upset?"

Drake stared at her. "Don't you get it? He couldn't just *kill* you; he had to make you a vampire. That was his final revenge on me."

"All right, so I'm a vampire. Is that so terrible?"

Drake realized the only honest answer would be incredibly rude. There was an uncomfortable pause. It felt like a first date, but infinitely more awkward.

She finally broke the silence. "So. How do I look?"

Horrified as he was, Drake couldn't lie. "Kinda...*wow*."

Nikki giggled, flattered. "No, I mean, literally: How do I look? 'Cause you know, the mirror thing?" Nikki pointed at his hall-tree mirror. Yep, only Drake was casting a reflection. Where Nikki ought to be in the glass, it was empty.

He looked back at her.

"Oh, right. Well, your hair is like, jet-black now. And you don't have much of a tan."

Helpfully, he plucked a dead leaf from the back of her hair. It was driving him crazy, and she never would have seen it.

Nikki looked down at herself. "Whoa! Did I always have a rack like this?" She took a deep breath and was amused to see how quickly Drake's gaze was riveted.

After a bit, he remembered where her eyes were. "Babe, I'm feeling real uncomfortable."

"Me, too," she replied. "Are you going to keep me on your porch all night?"

"If I ask you in, then you can enter any time you want after that."

"Yep. That's how it works. So what? I mean, you gave me your key months ago."

"Right. But back then, I didn't think you'd use it to drink my blood."

"Excuse me?" she said, offended.

"Well, that's what you mean to do, right?"

"No!" She thought about it for a second. "Well, actually, yes. Would that be so bad?"

Now it was Drake's turn to think for a second. "I guess not. I don't know what I have to live for without you anyway. Come on in."

He blinked—and literally, in that blink of an eye, the doorway was empty. What the hell? Had he been dreaming again?

Then he felt her breath on the back of his neck, cool as a breeze off a snow-capped mountain, giving him a shiver of delight. She was now behind him in the room. She slipped her arms around him and hugged him tight, pressing her cheek against his shoulder.

"Awww!" she cooed. "You miss me that much?"

"You have no idea. Here, put me out of my misery." Drake tilted his head back, exposing his jugular.

She shook her hair back and ran her tongue across her crimson lips.

"We'll get to the blood drinking part in a bit. But first, you and I are going to make up for lost time."

"What do you mean?"

"Well, waking up in a coffin buried six feet underground kind of liberates you from the way you used to think. I mean, the old Nicole, she'd have freaked out. She'd have lost it. But if you're undead, you don't think..." here she squeaked: "'Ooh, I'm trapped! Someone help me!'

"You think, 'I'm getting the hell out of this shithole.' And then whoosh! You're out. And then you think about all the *other* things you've wanted in your life, but you thought you couldn't, or shouldn't, do anything about."

"You mean...?"

She nodded slowly with a lascivious look. "First, while you're still warm—'cause now I'm kinda into that—we are going to make up for all the horizontal dancing we never got to do when I was alive."

"Come again?"

She nodded. "And again, and again, and—"

"Nicole..."

"Nikki," she whispered.

With that, she kissed him. Gently at first, but with inexorably rising passion.

"Nic—ki... You're cold." She felt like she'd just dried off from a chilly midnight dip.

"You'll heat me up, big boy," she smiled, grabbing him by his shirt and pulling him into a much, much longer kiss.

Then she ripped his shirt open. Buttons flew. She grabbed his butt and pulled him into her embrace. His mind was a delirious fog. It didn't matter whether this was real or a dream. He wanted her so much he didn't care what happened afterward.

But then Drake heard a sizzle, and Nikki shoved him off her.

"OWWW!" she howled. "What the fucking hell was that?"

Nikki looked at her chest and saw a small cross-shaped burn, still smoking.

Drake looked down, and realized he was had never taken off her little gold crucifix. "Babe, I'm sorry! I forgot I had this on!"

Nikki blew on her tiny scar. "I guess aloe isn't going to help this, is it?"

Then she looked over at Drake. "You're still wearing the cross I gave you?" She cocked her head at him, adoringly. "That is *so sweet!*" Then she added, "Do me a favor and dump it."

Drake obediently raised it over his head. Then he froze.

"Wait a minute, what am I doing?" He shook off the last of his grogginess.

Nikki glided closer.

He put the cross back on.

She stopped.

He lifted it off again, she came a step nearer, but he put it on again, and she stopped. He faked lifting it. She tried to take a step but stopped like she hit a wall.

"Drake! That's not funny!"

"I'm sorry, but I had to be sure it works."

"Why?"

"Because I can't let you kill me."

"But I'm thirsty! And you've got, like, eight pints! You're swimming in it. I promise, I won't drink all of you."

"You might get carried away. You're not exactly yourself."

She turned to go. "Well, if you're not going to let me have a drink, I'll have to find someone else."

He took her arm. "No! You can't do that. Promise me, you won't go hunting on your own. You can't kill anyone."

"Not even someone really bad?"

"No! Of course not!" exclaimed Drake.

"What if they're terminal?" she asked.

"You'd drink dying person blood?"

"Um...no, it does sound kinda gross."

Drake took her face in her hands. "Trust me. I'll look

after you. Just promise me, no killing. You'll lose your soul for good!"

"Honey, I'm dead. I'm *beyond* dead. My soul is lost already."

"No. No, it's not!"

Drake ran to his desk and grabbed the translated pages.

"This is from Zaar's book about *vlkodlaks*. The legend says as long as you don't kill anyone, you can be restored to life. Don't you see?"

Nikki shook her head, bewildered.

"By making you undead, that arrogant asshole screwed up! I've got a way to bring you back!"

Nikki glided near to read over his shoulder.

"Really?"

He ran his finger under the text. She followed along.

"This part: 'For the victim of the Vampire may avoid his Fate...'"

Her eyes wandered. Up his finger to his wrist, his arm...

"'...if the original Vampire be destroyed...'"

...across his shoulder, to his throat. She licked her lips. She leaned in close.

"'...before his victim kills another for blood.'"

Drake looked over to find her fangs an inch from his jugular.

"Hey!"

He held up the crucifix.

Nikki shrank back, pouting.

"But, Drake...I'm *sooo thirsty!*"

Drake headed for his fridge.

"And not for Evian. Or that nasty cranberry lemonade."

Drake turned back. "Well, how long do you think you could go without...drinking?"

Nikki moved towards him. "I need something now."

Drake took a step back. "Like, *now* now?"

Nikki moved closer, nodding. "Like, if you dropped that cross, I'd suck you up like a navel orange."

"Okay, get a hold of yourself—whoa!" he yelped, as he fell backwards over his chair.

20

A PERFECT EVENING

I T HAD BEEN A SLOW NIGHT AT THE EMERGENCY room.
The quiet ended when Drake staggered into the ER
lobby of Good Samaritan Hospital with a crimson-soaked
towel pressed to his neck.

"Somebody help me! I was attacked by...by some kind of
wild animal!" he rasped.

A young female doctor of Hindu extraction rushed out.

Drake was panting, weaving. "I'm so weak. Lost so much
blood..." Drake leaned on a chair, rubber-legged.

She turned to an orderly. "Get him onto a bed!"

The orderly half-carried Drake into the nearest exam
cubicle. The nurse wrapped a blood pressure cuff around
his arm.

"What's your name?" the doctor asked.

"Uh...Kevin," said Drake.

"Take it easy, Kevin, we're going to get you all fixed up.
Do you know your blood type?"

"O-positive."

"O-negative," said Nikki.

The nurse whirled, startled: A bizarrely pale woman in a

white wedding dress was standing with them in the exam room, though the nurse would have sworn there'd been no one else there a second ago.

Drake gave Nikki a quizzical look. She touched her tummy and silently mouthed, *"Just got a craving."*

Drake gave her a severe look, but turned to the doctor. "Yeah, sorry. O-negative."

An admitting clerk brought in a clipboard full of forms. "We need you to fill these out."

"I'll do it," volunteered Nikki.

Drake groaned and slumped back onto the bed. The doctor turned to the nurse. "Get two units of O-neg, stat!"

The clerk handed Nikki the clipboard, then withdrew. The nurse hopped to it.

The doctor tried to pry Drake's red-soaked towel from his neck, but he put up a desperate struggle.

"Kevin...Kevin, come on now...you're going to have to let me take a look."

"No, no, I can't, I'll bleed out!" cried Drake, clamping the towel to his throat with grim determination.

The nurse returned with two thick plastic bags of dark maroon blood. Suddenly, screams erupted from the waiting area.

Not screams of pain—these were pure fright. Panicked people yelling for help. The nurse instinctively ran to the source. The doctor ran after her, trying to grab her.

"Where are you going, we've got a—"

The words died in the doctor's throat at seeing a roomful of ER patients running this way and that, fleeing something black and enormous that was flapping over their heads.

"Call 9-1-1!" the doctor yelled at the admitting clerk, who had ducked below her desk. "Tell them we have a bat loose and it could be rabid!" Then she grabbed the nurse's arm and dragged her back to the exam area.

But their patient was gone. So was the woman who had been handed the clipboard. And so were the blood bags. All that was left was a towel soaked with what smelled like a combination of cranberry lemonade and ketchup.

———

Mike Hanna was busting his ass for the couple at the patio table; yet somehow, he sensed he was going to wind up getting stiffed.

Mike had been counting on this: The guy had made the reservation a week before, which normally meant a romantic dinner. Maybe even a proposal. In this case, the guy had told Mike it was the their last date as an unmarried couple before their wedding. Tip potential: Huge.

But these emotional milestones could be tricky. Sometimes the pressure on the relationship could be so intense, that instead of a love-filled evening, you got a nasty public breakup with both diners storming off in opposite directions. The twenty-percent tip would be the first casualty. In extreme cases, they'd forget to pay the check, period.

On the plus side, Christophe's was located in a classic old brick building off Los Feliz Boulevard; it was famed for its funky courtyard and its chef's way with seafood and lamb. On the minus side, it had no beer or wine license. The bistro provided the stemware; the diners brought their own alcohol. That would lower the total bill and thus, Mike's tip.

But this patron had seemed like a real romantic. When he had made the reservation, he slipped Mike an extra ten to buy a single long-stemmed rose at the florist next door, to present to his lady-love when she sat down at the appointed hour.

Mike being Mike, he'd decided, why cut the florist in? He knew of a spot where wild roses grew in abundance in a shady dell in nearby Griffith Park, so he'd clipped one that morning.

But the evening of romance started to go south as soon as they sat down and Mike handed the lady her rose. Instead of blushing or gushing, she sat there paralyzed, stiff as a board.

"Drake, I can't move!"

"Okay, don't panic."

"Should I call the paramedics?" asked Mike.

"No!"

The guy plucked the rose from his girl's hand, wound up, and hurled it like a javelin into the boulevard. A passing SUV immediately pressed it flat enough for her memory book, if she didn't mind tire marks.

The lady took a breath and relaxed.

Her date glared at Mike. "What kind of rose was that? Where'd you buy it?"

"Well, to be honest, they grow wild up in the park."

"If I'd wanted a *wild* rose, I'd have asked you for one!" said the guy, exasperated.

"I-I'm sorry," stammered Mike.

"Forget it. You didn't know," said the guy.

"Can you just bring us some glasses?" asked the bride-to-be, who definitely looked parched.

Mike hustled into the restaurant, got a couple of menus and two wine glasses, and swept back to the table with them. Then, determined to salvage his big tip, he hurried into the kitchen.

Twelve seconds later, Mike served a steaming breadbasket with extra garlic puffs. He threw back the cloth to let the savory aroma drift to their nostrils and whet their appetites.

"On the house!" grinned Mike.

"Ulllppp," said the lady, clamping a hand to her mouth, half a second from projectile vomiting.

"Get these things out of here! We don't want any garlic, on anything!" snapped the guy, pushing the basket back at Mike.

Jeez, thought Mike, carrying the rejected puffs back inside. What was *their* deal? Was it a full moon or something?

Maybe, Mike thought, she's got stomach flu. But if so, why were they eating at an outdoor table on a chilly night in October? And her in that sheer dress? Or maybe she had morning sickness. That might explain the impending wedding. She did look awful pale.

Mike checked his hair in the big mirror that ran the length of the wall behind the bar. Hair was good. Audition tomorrow.

Maybe he should offer them a seat inside? He went out.

"No!" they both shouted in unison.

Mike sighed and left them to read their menus. She wasn't reading. Probably on a diet, going to order a salad.

He could kiss his tip good-bye, Mike figured. He debated whether to spit in their desserts.

He looked out the window and saw the guy opening a beer. Man, thought Mike, these two redefine the word 'cheap'.

What was worse was the bride was filling her wine glass under the table. From a plastic bag.

Nikki and Drake strolled down the cemetery road, laughing merrily. The debacle at Chez Christophe was hours behind them, and they had to admit, in retrospect, it was pretty damn funny.

"Oh, man, the look on his face when I couldn't move," giggled Nikki. "I did feel bad for him. I guess he never read Bram Stoker."

Drake was chuckling. "Yeah, we should clue him in about the paralyzing effects of a wild rose on undead patrons." Then Drake realized, "Oh, crap. I forgot his tip. Poor guy."

"Literally, thanks to you," noted Nikki.

They chortled.

"Well, already he pocketed my ten bucks for the rose. He coulda done worse," allowed Drake.

Nikki nodded. "He could've had a bat dive-bomb him."

Drake cracked up. "God, you totally should have done that!"

They were off on another laughing jag, until they had to lean against each other, catching their breath.

Then they walked on, quiet for a time.

Finally, Drake couldn't stand it, he had to ask. "Did you really have a craving for O-negative? I mean, how would you even know what that tastes like?"

She chuckled. "Naah. Just messin' with you."

Nikki squeezed the last of the blood bag into her wine glass and drained it.

"Ahhh. That really hit the spot. Thanks for dinner, Drake."

Drake stifled a shudder.

Nikki noticed. "What?"

"Nothing."

"C'mon, Drake. Spill."

"Don't say spill."

Nikki slumped. "I knew it. The blood drinking *does* bother you."

"No, no. Well, a little. It's just...I was hoping the stemware would help, but I think it actually made it worse."

Nikki looked at the glass. The dregs in the bottom were starting to coagulate.

"Well, a girl's gotta drink!" she protested.

Drake put his arm around her. "I know, babe. It takes some getting used to. But you and I both know it's not permanent." He forced extra conviction into his tone. She needed to believe him.

They continued in silence for a moment, and then Nikki stopped and pointed downward. "Oh, this is me."

He looked at the brand-new stone plaque in the grass.

NICOLE FINLEY

Somewhere in the distance, a cock crowed. Which of course meant that soon someone would get a notice they were in violation of the municipal code. You're not allowed to keep roosters in Los Angeles.

Nikki handed Drake the glass. "Well, back to the old boneyard. You know what the sun would do to this complexion. Oh, almost forgot this." Nikki slid off her gold engagement ring with the little blue sapphire and handed it to Drake.

He took her hand. "I'll bring this back. I'll bring *you* back. I'll find Zaar and destroy him."

"How? His coffin's not here anymore."

"I just have to figure out where he hid it. As I said, I can think of one likely spot right off. So if I'm not here at sundown..."

"I know where to go."

Drake looked at Nikki's grave and heaved a sigh. "I hate to think of you down there."

Nikki smiled and shook her head. "It's funny. It feels like I've had a long day, and I'm coming home on a cold night, and now I'll slip into bed, pull the covers over my head, and sleep...warm and snug and safe."

"Really?" He looked at the grave, imagining six feet of earth over his own head, and shuddered.

She gave his hand a reassuring squeeze. "I had a great time tonight, Drake."

"Me, too."

He covered the crucifix with his hand to be sure it wouldn't touch her exposed skin, then kissed her.

Her lips felt soft and cool on his. After a moment, he realized she wasn't there. In her place was a thick, cold cloud of mist that drifted down into the soil atop her grave, just as dawn broke over the Hollywood Hills.

ACKNOWLEDGMENTS

My gratitude for reading, notes, proofing, suggestions, kind words or invaluable advice, to:

Bobbie Metevier, Christiana Miller, Steven Paul Leiva, Tery Lopez, Kim Myers, Steve Chivers, Jack & Carole Mendelsohn, Kimmi Baecker, Deirdre Molitor, Jim Casaburi, Randall William Cook, Graham Flashner, Michael Ray Brown, Shelly Goldstein, Bart Gold, Dan Fiorella, Beth Szymkowski, Lisa Kors, Ron Zwang, Andrew Nordvall, Brenda Pontiff, Devon Schwartz, Arthur Tiersky, Art Eisenson, Kelvin Wyles, Elizabeth Cadwalader, Mike Moberly, Dan Dobrin, Lee Rose Emery, Ashley McCluskey, Joshua Cossey at Alamo Jewelry & Loan, and Deacon Ron Butler.

Glenn Camhi, for keen eye, steady hand and infinite patience.

Deepest thanks to Mickey Galef, Barry and Ellen, Mary and Richard. Also Steve Hayes, Robin Stein, Gary Black, Marty Rudoy, David Larmore, Ian Abrams, Katherine Fugate, friends indeed.

Sue and Deirdre, for enduring another book.

ABOUT THE AUTHOR

DOUG MOLITOR is an L.A. native who has written for comedies (*Sledge Hammer!, Lohman & Barkley, You Can't Take It With You, Police Academy*) and sci-fi/fantasy adventure series (*Sliders, Mission: Genesis, Adventure Inc., Young Hercules, F/X*) and the western comedy *Lucky Luke*.

In animation, he was co-writer of the feature *SpacePOP*, and writer and/or story editor for over 200 episodes of such series as *The Wizard of Oz, Happily Ever After, X-Men, The Future Is Wild, Bill & Ted's Excellent Adventures, Sinbad, Where on Earth is Carmen Sandiego?, Class of the Titans, Roswell Conspiracies, Sabrina, Beetlejuice* and *Captain Planet*. For the latter, he won two Environmental Media Awards and was nominated for the Humanitas Prize. His 2008 musical election spoof, with Hillary and Obama singing "Anything You Can Do, I Can Do Better" had 2.4 million hits on YouTube.

Doug is also a former *Jeopardy* Champ, appearing a total of 13 days on two versions of the show.

To be notified of Doug's next book, please send your email address to TheAltadenaPress@gmail.com

You can also connect with him on social media or on the website thealtadenapress.com

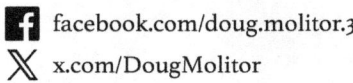 facebook.com/doug.molitor.3
x.com/DougMolitor

EXCERPT FROM FULL MOON FEVER: PURE SILVER

CHAPTER ONE: REVELATION

F ATHER KEVIN FINLEY HAD BEEN HEARING confessions all morning. If he himself had anything to confess right now, it was that he'd had it up to here with these pious people and their piddling moral misdemeanors. They had to be holding back. Not a good, juicy sin in the bunch.

The church had emptied out. He was about a minute from switching off the green light on the booth that showed he was available. Then what he prayed would be his last penitent of the day clumped into the other compartment.

The priest slid open the screen.

From the other side came a low, whispery voice, like Clint Eastwood had come in to do penance.

"Bless me, Father, for I have sinned."

"How long has it been since your last confession?"

"Thirteen years."

"What is the nature of your sins?"

"I took the Lord's name a lot, and I blasphemed. I stole a book. Also a car."

Father Kevin was sure this wasn't a member of his congregation, but these sins sounded oddly familiar.

"Is there anything else?"

"I kissed a vampire. Who's my dead fiancée."

Now he knew the voice. The burly young priest stood up instantly, banging his head on the top of the booth. "Drake?!"

It had been thirteen years since Drake Callahan had seen his pal Kevin this furious, so he kept the baptismal font between them as he explained his reasons.

"I know how insane this sounds. But you of all people, should believe me, Kevin. This is your field! Resurrection, demonic possession—it's all in the Gospels."

"Oho, very clever, Drake. But I believe in God, not the bogeyman!"

"You guys do exorcisms, don't you?"

"Virtually never. Only when the church has indisputable proof that can't be explained otherwise."

"Well, I have proof."

"Oh, really?" said Father Kevin, folding his arms.

"You know how a vampire doesn't show up in a mirror, or a photograph?"

"Yeah, yeah, I watched the same stupid monster movies you did."

Drake showed Kevin a picture on his cell phone. Kevin peered at it, then looked at Drake, bewildered. "This is a photo of your couch."

Drake leaned toward him, dramatic. "Nikki was sitting right on it when I took the picture."

Kevin nodded. "I am going to punch you so hard. And since when do you call Nicole 'Nikki'?"

"She said she prefers it."

"My sister is dead, you bastard!"

"She is, yes. But she also spent last night with me. She's not exactly the same girl you grew up with."

"Get out of my church, right now!" said Kevin, his face reddening.

Drake shoved his hand into his pocket. "Okay, Doubting Thomas. I didn't want to do this, but...here." Drake grabbed Kevin's hand, turned it palm up, and slapped Nicole's sapphire ring on it. "You helped her get this sized, remember?"

Kevin's angry scowl stretched into astonishment. He put the golden band right up to his eye. He gasped, even more impressed than Drake expected.

"What?"

"It has the scratch from when she dropped it."

"What scratch? She didn't tell me that."

"She cried and made me promise not to tell you." Kevin's voice quavered. "This was on her finger when we sealed her casket. I saw her buried. I was at her grave just an hour ago. It hasn't been touched. Drake...how in God's name did you get this?"

"You mean, how did a solid ring pass through six feet of dirt over her coffin without disturbing a blade of grass? It's physically impossible, Kev. Unless everything I just told you about Peter Zaar becoming a vampire, and turning Nicole into one, is true."

Read the rest of the story in
Full Moon Fever: Pure Silver